Jubilee Sunset Romance

Deborah McDonald

ISBN: 978-1-954693-01-2

FV 12

Printed in the United States

This is the first book in the Over the Bay Series.

www.IntellectPublishing.com

Acknowledgments

It's exciting to write my first book. I would like to thank my family for supporting me with their patience as I spent many hours burning the midnight oil at the computer and so glad you all know how to sleep through my clicking of the keys on the laptop at 2 AM. Emma, Amanda, Eva and Olivia, I think you are all wonderful and have an amazing future ahead. You are true ladies and we are so proud of you all. To my husband, who's a great dad to all the girls. Thank you, Owen, for all of your support, sense of humor and love throughout the years (Getting engaged at Beaver Pond was one of the highlights of all our years together). Gwen, Zoey and Kuma, I appreciate the times you dogs have kept me company while I type on the computer. (I think you were really hoping for a treat, but that's a story for another time.)

Thank you to my siblings Linda, Paul and Laurie and all of the fun trips to NOLA. Here's to many more in the future. To the family in what I like to call the other part of the SEC! Thanks for the football texting Saturdays, the jokes and birthday wishes!

Thank you to my collaborator/editor, Deborah Navarro. She has brought so much to this book with ideas for dialogue and frequent checks on grammar/punctuation. I love her idioms! She has been a good friend over the years. She's just amazing.

Emma, thanks for being the first reader of the book and helping to edit the first draft. I was able to look at relationships in a whole new light with your advice. Thank you to Julia Taylor, for the fabulous book cover. You are a true artist!

Thank you to my oldest friends, who have stuck with me, eaten with me, celebrated with me, gone to events with me, and listened to me talk A LOT over the years! You know who you are!

To my dear high school friend, who has helped me and been my friend for years. They made the energizer bunny with you in mind. You are always taking care of your family and having three things going on at one time and you take it in stride. Thanks for caring for others, always!

Thanks to all who answered questions about medical procedures, jubilees and Mobile Bay! Any mistakes are my own! Thanks Maddi for the Halloween scene!

Thanks to the Little Flower friends who loved my mother and continue to include our family in your church and community! To our friends who are family, thanks for the good times!

To memories of Father Oliver Adams and my family's time spent over the bay growing up in the 70's and 80's. Much of what I wrote about the bay were from my memories of catching crabs in traps, staying at the bay house in Mullet Point and my mother making gumbo with crab bodies! The cylinder block house still stands today! I learned about sleeping on a wharf and being part of a jubilee! Those were great years with nothing but the bay breeze blowing through the windows and maybe a box fan for comfort as there was no air conditioning and no washer/dryer! To the friend that had the pier with the hammock! That inspired a great scene!

Thank you to the members of the Pensters! What a great

group of writers! Thank you John O'Melveny Woods,

Ron, Frank and Alan for answering questions! Thank you Rosalie for the many emails answered and meeting me to answer even more questions. What a wealth of talent in the Pensters!

Jubilee Sunset Romance

Chapter 1

As Florence looked up at the gate surrounding the theme park office, she took a moment to take a deep breath. She smoothed down her honey blonde hair which was not in its usual ponytail and the apple green sleeveless dress she was wearing which was not her usual attire. It was the month of July in Alabama, which meant scorching heat and humidity. She longed to be sitting out on her back porch in a t-shirt and shorts, but she needed this job.

She pushed open the gate to Jubilee Sunset Theme Park. It was quiet here at the front, where the offices were located. She was due to see a Mr. Simmons, the owner and overseer for the park.

As she opened the front door to the office building, a blast of cool air was a much welcome respite from the heat.

"May I help you?"

Florence looked up and saw an older woman approach her. She couldn't help but notice the beautiful mahogany skin and a figure to die for in a crisp linen suit with matching shoes.

Florence nodded, "I'm here about the educator position and have an interview with Mr. Simmons."

The woman said, "I'm Toni McGregor, the administrator of

the park. I will be interviewing you today. Mr. Simmons is not available at the moment. Won't you follow me?"

Florence walked through the lobby and couldn't help but smile at the decor---old pictures of carnival rides and circus animals hung on the walls, with comfortable chairs lining the areas perfect for sitting and staring at the pictures: a man walking a tightrope, a huge elephant throwing water on his back, roller coasters, and a picture of a clown that ran from the ceiling to the floor.

"Here we are Miss…I don't believe I caught your name."
"Oh, sorry. It's Florence Smith. Please take a seat, Miss Smith."

Florence looked around the room and back at Ms. McGregor with questioning eyes, "Yes, Miss Smith, there's a rowboat in the middle of our office. Just step into it and sit on the bench in the middle. If you look around you will notice that this is the Jubilee Room."

Florence noticed scads of pictures and informational signs lining the walls of various stages of fish being caught, pictures of captains she recognized from story books and photos of jubilees that took place on the Eastern Shore of Mobile Bay.

Ms. McGregor asked her if she had ever seen a jubilee. Florence shook her head, "No ma'am, I don't believe I have."

"You would have remembered it. It's quite the spectacle. You will find that through our offices and even the park itself Mr. Simmons likes to use items and decor that show off our southern area."

As Florence seated herself, she said, "You have a full-time job opening for a children's educator in the park." Florence handed her resume over, "I've been an Elementary teacher for 6 years now. I have my master's degree and have worked with children in afterschool programs as well. I've worked in summer camps every summer: Boys and Girls Club, camps for children with special needs, and church camps. I'm looking for something different out of the classroom and feel that I would be right for this position. I also live in Daphne, which is not far from here."

Florence watched Ms. McGregor scan her resume and look at her.

"Well, you certainly seem qualified, but let me ask you one thing Miss Smith. What do you do for fun?"

"What do I do for fun ma'am?"

"Yes, when you're not working, what do you do for fun?"

She had a hard time answering as she worked year around to help take care of her mother and sister. As Ms. McGregor looked at her, Florence could only think of one thing that came even close, "I like to dance."

Ms. McGregor leaned forward and asked, "Dance? Did you have formal lessons? What type of dance?"

Florence described the city recreation activity center that she went to growing up.

"My sister and I took lessons from a volunteer dance teacher. She taught us ballet, tap, jazz and um….disco."

Ms. McGregor raised an eyebrow and stared at Florence. At that moment, a troop of cub scouts came flying into the room, sounding for all the world like gulls at the pier arguing over scraps of bait. Florence couldn't help but smile at the energy in the room. The kids were jumping up and down. She noticed one little boy shying away from the noise. He was covering his ears. In the midst of the boys was a clown holding a bunch of balloons.

Ms. McGregor said hello to the clown and grinned. The

clown smiled from ear to ear. He looked around him, "Ok, kids, I hope you had a great time today at the park. Everyone gets a balloon and a grab bag." The kids jumped up and down with excitement. Florence noticed the little boy continued to cover his ears. She happened to see a pair of new earbuds in a basket on the desk and looked at Ms. McGregor who nodded.

Florence stood very quietly and gave them to the little boy, who put them in his ears. He smiled at Florence. Florence smiled back. She gave him a fist bump.

An assistant appeared in the doorway. The clown handed over the balloons, "Ms. Green, would you mind getting our guests today a grab bag and one of these balloons? Their troop leaders are waiting in the front atrium. Kids, what do you say to Bongo the Clown for your day at the park?"

They jumped up and down with choruses of "Thank you!" and fist bumps with the clown took place as the kids left. The boy with the earbuds was the last to leave. He looked up at the clown as the clown quietly looked at him. He gave the clown a fist bump and the clown smiled as the boy joined the rest of the kids.

As the clown turned back, he zeroed in on Florence. Florence noticed he had the most beautiful blue eyes she had ever seen and even with the baggy clown suit on, he looked to be in really good shape. Now, where did that thought come from?

"Ms. McGregor, who do we have here?"

"Riley, this is Florence Smith, who is applying for the educator position." He stuck out his hand and she rose to shake his hand and jumped as a buzzer went off.

"Sorry," he chuckled, "the kids love the hand buzzer." He removed the buzzer from his hand sheepishly, "Let's try that again."

As they shook hands, Florence asked, "So you're one of the clowns here?" Ms. McGregor laughed, "You can say that again!"

Florence gave her a puzzled look as Riley just grinned. "I'm covering for our regular clown."

Ms. McGregor said, "Yes, Riley is our go-to guy for a lot of things around here." He sat on the edge of Ms. McGregor's desk and asked," Are you a teacher?"

"Yes, just looking for a different setting to work with children."

Riley paused, "You couldn't have picked a better place and the boss is a great guy! I've known him for years."

Ms. McGregor smiled.

Riley quieted down, "So, you like kids, hmm?"

Florence looked at Ms. McGregor and then back at the clown. "Yes, yes I do. I was actually one myself once."

He snickered, "That helps."

Ms. McGregor asked him if there was anything else he needed.

"No, I think I have all I need."

Those blue eyes lasered in on Florence. She managed not to squirm underneath that gaze.

Riley raised a hand, "Miss Smith, good luck with the job," and he then left quietly.

Florence turned back to Ms. McGregor and noticed she was staring at her. She waited. "Ok, Miss Smith. I will contact references and if all checks out, I say the job is yours. I will be in touch."

As Florence left the building, she couldn't help but feel relieved. She could help her mom and help her sister pay for school. She turned to look back at the park before she left. She noticed several families smiling, laughing together and kids without a care in the world. Florence took a deep breath. What she had said to the clown wasn't the whole truth. Yes, she had been a kid once, but unfortunately, not for long.

Several miles away at the Mobile County Jail, a barrel-chested man with a long scar on his pockmarked face and tattoos on his arms and neck was quietly thinking. Jerry Smith laid on his cot in his cell and thought about how he got there. All he had done was try to take care of those snot nose kids and sister in law when his brother died. But did they thank him? Hell, no. He had been in jail for 18 years now and for what!

"So, what if I knocked them around some? Kids need to have sense knocked into them, especially when they get loud. All I asked for was to have supper on the table when I got home from the plant. Was that too much to ask for when I let them live in my house? So what if I drank and smoked a few cigarettes in the house. It was my house!"

A hard-working man deserved a beer or two after a day of work. His sister-in-law was always preaching to him not to drink around the kids and not to smoke in the house. It was his damn house. Even the oldest brat, Florence, used to tell him to stop smoking and once she even threw his cigarettes away. He got even with her. A few cigarette burns on her back stopped that nonsense. Couldn't leave the marks where schoolteachers would notice it. So, he had to be smart. He was always the smart one,

So when my sister-in-law griped at me, I'd knock her

around. It certainly shut her up where she wouldn't say anything. Damn kids too. They sure got quiet. I was just trying to teach them some manners. Damn brother was too soft on them."

Jerry wasn't afraid to do what needed to be done. Hell, he'd even killed a man one time when the man cheated him during a pool game at a local bar. He was lying in wait for the man on a deserted dirt road when unfortunately, the man staggered into the woods to take a leak. He never saw it coming and his body would never be found. Jerry knew how to take care of business. He'd been up for parole several times now but that brat, Florence, and the cop that put him here would always tell the parole board how he should never see the light of day after the abuse of those kids and sister- in- law.

"If I ever get out, they'll find that I always take care of business. They won't know what hit them until it's too late."

He leaned back in his cot and smiled.

Chapter 2

Riley Simmons, minus the clown costume, stuck his head back into Toni's office, "Well, what did you think?" asked Riley.

Toni looked at her boss with the bright blue eyes, brown hair a little long on the collar, year-round tan, with an angel's face. He was now dressed in the customary uniform of the park---a red t-shirt with the park logo of a fish jumping in the middle of the sun and the words Jubilee Sunset Theme Park encircled the logo. He wore a pair of khaki shorts with his custom beat up Nike tennis shoes. If she'd been twenty-five years younger, she might have looked in his direction, as handsome as he was.

She sighed, "Everything I have on her indicates that she is bright and has worked with children in a variety of settings. She has 2 teaching degrees and stellar performance reviews from her principal and colleagues. She mentioned a sister but didn't say much else about any other family or anything personal. You know how some people want to tell you their life story, but she kept it professional."

Riley leaned against the wall, "Anything else?"

"Yes, I liked how she helped out the little boy earlier."

Riley had noticed that as well, "She seems like a natural around kids. How do you think she'd get along with the staff?"

"Well, that remains to be seen. We try to hire smart, caring people without the drama.

We can't always be 100% drama free, but we come close."

"Okay. Let's go for it. Today's Friday, how about we start her on Monday?"

Toni waited a beat and said, "Are you going to meet with her and let her know her boss is a clown?"

"Very funny Toni. I'll get around to it. By the way, did she say what she liked to do for fun? Any hobbies?"

"She seemed taken aback for a minute when I asked her." "Well, what did she say?" asked Riley.

"Are you ready for this? She likes to dance." Riley paused. "Yeah, thought you'd like that Mr. Showman." Toni said, "She apparently took some classes when she was younger with her sister. That's how I know she has a sibling. I get the feeling she didn't have much as a child. She mentioned a city activity center with a volunteer dance instructor. She certainly looks like a dancer….in shape. I wish I'd had a pair of great legs like she does when I was her age."

"Huh," Riley said, "didn't notice." Toni stared at Riley. He grinned. He told Toni goodnight and went to survey the crowds still in the park. What he told Toni wasn't quite accurate. He had noticed Florence Smith the minute he stepped into the room.

He thought of the letter his Uncle Frank wrote to him when he left him the park in his will.

Pick the right people you want to work in the park. You're going to be working your ass off 24/7, so you need to be able to live with your decisions on who you hire. You want to be around people you actually like working with and who like working for you. Treat your employees like family, tell them what you expect and usually that will do the trick. Treat others with kindness and that's what you'll get in return. Respect women always because they are smarter than us and they get the job done. Can't really give you advice about not getting involved with someone you work with because as you well remember I met your Aunt Alice when she worked as a dancer in the park.

Prettiest girl I ever met and fell in love with her the first time I saw her. She put me off for an entire year saying she didn't want people talking, didn't want other employees treating her differently, didn't think it looked right. Never saw a better dancer than her, even Ginger Rogers, and you know she was my favorite. That first year, Alice had pulled muscles and sprained her ankle. She almost fell off the Mother's Day float she was riding on in the park. She was tough as nails and just kept going because she loved to dance and loved the park. I think I told you the story of when she was helping me do a test run on the Ferris wheel late one night when everyone had gone home. I had used the remote to get us up there and we were sitting side by side. I told her about all the gray hairs she gave me this past year with her "almost accidents". She leaned over, moved her hands up my chest and said, "Here's to one more gray hair." And then she kissed me. That was our first kiss and I never forgot it.

It took her a long time to realize that people we worked with had become family. They knew how we felt about each other and were our biggest cheerleaders. Be smart, use your head, but also follow your heart. Or you will lose out on the best moments of your life. If you are reading this letter, then that means I am gone. But remember, your Aunt Alice and I had many wonderful years together and I loved every one of them, even when times were tough.

Take care of the park for me. I know you're ready because you were my shadow all these years, going back to when you were young and thought I needed to build TreeHouse City as part of the park because everyone liked tree houses right? Aunt Alice loved teaching you how to sing and to dance. She loved spending time with you. I love you like you were my own son, and I am sorry your dad died at such an early age. We had fun running the park. He was a wonderful man, much like you have grown to be. He loved you and your mom.

He would be very proud of the man you've become. Remember, I love you son and say hello to your Aunt Alice for me. Dance with her in the park for old time's sake. But be careful, she's getting up there in age and I don't want her spraining an ankle--(and don't tell her I said that). If she ever heard a remark like that from me, she'd make me bunk on the couch.

Love,

Your Uncle Frank

Riley had loved the old man too. He wiped his eyes as he realized where thoughts of his uncle had left him. He looked up and there it was…. TreeHouse City. His uncle and dad actually had listened to his thoughts when he was little and had built TreeHouse City. Well, it was more like 8 tree houses that could be explored, and kids had loved it. They had made it safe with stairs instead of ladders and there was even an elevator in two of them, so that people who couldn't walk could reach the top floor of the house. His dad and Uncle were ahead of their time in wanting every person to have an enjoyable experience in the park.

He remembered the night his uncle and dad had taken him up to stay in one of those treehouses one night after the park had closed for the evening. They had brought sandwiches, cookies, and a thermos of cold sweet tea his mom had put together for them to munch on during the night. To change with the times, Riley had the treehouses converted as a place families and guests could rent as part of accommodations at the park. Each treehouse was furnished with a kitchen, two bedrooms, a pull-out sofa, and a bathroom.

He looked up to heaven and thanked his dad and uncle for what they had given him.

He walked to his bungalow that had a private entrance in the back of the park. He loved the palm trees and foliage in the front of the bungalow and looked towards the 4 other bungalows down from his that had been built back when his Uncle and dad had started the park and needed to be on site quickly. They had offered the other bungalows to trusted family and friends. One of those trusted friends was sitting on the stoop in the bungalow next to his nursing a cold beer.

He walked over to his best friend since childhood who was his partner in those TreeHouse City adventures, Dr. George Huntington, or Hunt for short.

He was a doctor in the local urgent care during the week but spent his weekends as the doctor on call at the park. He always reminded Riley of a young Jimmy Stewart, a little on the thin side and a nice guy, "Well, Riley, how was your day? Take a load off," he said to Riley as Hunt pointed to space on the stoop next to him.

Riley sat and Hunt handed over a cold bottle of beer, "Don't mind if I do. Thanks Hunt." Riley took a long drink. "Oh man, that's good. Oh, my day. Let's see. I was up at the crack of dawn 'cuz one of the gates wouldn't open to the entrance of the park when an employee tried to get in, and Fred from maintenance had to be here so we got that working. Then one of the electronic ticket machines went out and our 'tech genius' Rafael was all over that and got it running.

Hunt glanced at his best friend and said, "Man, you had a day!"

"Oh, yeah. Wait for the rest of it. We weren't sure we were going to take the steamboat out today due to bad weather. But saints preserve us, it moved further away from us. You know how Captain Carl is about that boat."

"Oh yeah," Hunt said, "He loves to take that boat out and spin his tales for the guests. Hates to be grounded, mostly likes to talk about his days running the paddle boat down the Mississippi. I imagine he was a trip running that boat. Betcha he saw a thing or two on that river."

"Yep," Riley said, "Glad he and Cheryl were ready to move closer to the grandkids here, and he wasn't ready to hang up his captain's hat yet. You won't find a better, more safety conscious captain anywhere. He knows every inch of that boat. Won't let anyone clean it or touch it unless he's on deck supervising. Let's see, what else?"

Hunt speaks up, "There's more?"

"Oh, I got to dress up as a clown today. Herman was sick with the flu."

"Make-up, floppy shoes and all?" asked Hunt.

"Yep, and that's not even the best part," Riley grinned.

"Are you going to leave me hanging or are you going to tell me what's got you all happy as sunshine?"

"Well, there's a new lady coming on as the educator."

"Oh, a teacher.... Why would that make you so happy? You've had educators for years in the park. What makes this one so special? Wait, does she look like Reese Witherspoon? Please tell me Reese Witherspoon is going to work for us." Hunt had a thing for Reese Witherspoon ever since he saw her star in the movie with Moon in the title back when she was younger in the early 90's.

"No, sorry man. But she's very pretty. Honey blonde hair, great pair of legs, and I caught a sense of humor there. Plus, she was good with one of the kids in my group today, so it's a win-win. And wait for it, she's a dancer."

Hunt looked up and said, "Aw, Aunt Alice would really like to hear that." He smiled fondly, because if he couldn't have Reese Witherspoon, he always had Aunt Alice.

She'd been a real looker back in the day and he still thought she was one beautiful lady.

He clinked his beer to Riley's and said, "Here's to Aunt Alice." They lapsed into a comfortable silence.

Hunt mused, "Didn't they teach you in that fancy business college you went to not to date employees?"

Riley looked Hunt's way and said, "I'm not dead yet, and I always appreciate a beautiful woman. But, yeah, you're right. I won't put this park in jeopardy. It means too much to me."

"So," Hunt asked, "where does that leave you?"

"Well, I guess hanging out with you and drinking beer most nights."

"To quote Uncle Frank," Hunt said, "there are worse things that could happen."

Chapter 3

The next day, Riley was experiencing one of the worst things that could happen in a theme park. A car had hit a pole off the I-10 interstate and power was out for several miles. Thankfully, no one was injured in the wreck and power was restored an hour before the park opened. Then one of the large freezers broke down in one of the restaurants in the park, but thanks to Fred, it was up and running with no food spoilage. He owed that man a raise.

He also reunited a child with his lost parents. He cautioned a group of teenagers who were a little too zealous about wanting to run through the park to get to their next ride. The Salute to America float had broken down before the mid-morning parade, but thanks to their float crew it was up and running. Despite all the headaches, Riley loved every minute of it. It was exhausting work, and while he had employees he trusted to fix any problem that arose, he liked to keep his hand in. He still walked the park every morning and night, just like his uncle and dad had done when they opened the park.

As Riley turned the corner in the Wild, Wild West section for a bottle of water, his eye caught on a group of young kids listening to the newly hired educator, Florence Smith.

He walked closer to hear her telling the kids about the Wild

West Days of Billy the Kid, Wild Bill Hickok, and Calamity Jane. Riley listened intently as Florence told the group about the confinement of Geronimo in Mount Vernon for seven years.

"Ok kids," said Florence." If you step right this way, you will see Cowboy Gene lasso a wooden horse. Notice this line of wooden horses behind me? He will show you how to lasso your own horse." A chorus of whoops and cheers were heard from the group.

One of the girls in the group said, "Miss Smith, even girls get a turn, right?"

"Oh, yes ma'am, Miss Frances. Everyone gets a turn." Florence then produced 10 small cowboy hats and asked Frances to hand them out to all the kids in her group.

Florence looked up at Cowboy Gene, "Okay, Cowboy Gene, they're all yours!" "Well, Miss Smith, that was impressive."

As Florence took a swig of water and turned around, she came face to face with a young John Ritter. But it couldn't be. Her favorite actor had unfortunately died far too soon. A college friend had introduced her to his movies and old reruns of Three's Company. Then she zeroed in on the bright blue eyes, "Riley, the clown, right? Not in costume today?"

Riley chuckled, looked down at his park emblem shirt and said, "Not today."

"Oh," Florence said, "so you're a visitor today at the park, just seeing the sights?"

"Something like that. How is your first day at the park?

Florence looked at the group of kids, still working with Cowboy Gene and said, "So far so good. I've been working on the program and still making lesson plans. That never goes away."

"I'm glad to hear that. Where are you from, Miss Smith?"

"Call me Florence please."

"Okay, Florence, did you grow up around here?" Riley inquired.

"Yes, I grew up in Mobile. How about you?"

Riley grinned and said, "Yes, not far from here. Any sisters or brothers?" Riley asked this to see if she would share this information with him.

Florence hesitated, "I have one sister, younger than me, who's in college at the University of South Alabama." Then Florence looked down at her shoes.

Riley thought, "Toni was right. Florence doesn't say much about family, only what I asked. Most people if I asked them would talk nonstop about family. Looks like Florence isn't one of those people."

At that moment, a scream was heard behind them. Young Frances had caught herself a wooden horse. Frances ran up to Florence and Riley.

"Nice job, Miss Frances," Florence exchanged a high five with Frances, "Miss Frances, this is Mr. Riley. He's a clown in the park."

Riley raised his eyebrows, smiled, and thought that's how his mom would describe him. Riley waved to Frances and said, "Well, hello Miss Frances. I hope you're having fun."

She looked up at Riley and exclaimed, "Wow, you have the prettiest blue eyes. Are they real?"

Florence looked away but not before Riley caught a big grin spreading across her face. Riley said, "Yes ma'am, at least that's what my mom told me. I've had people ask me that all of my life."

Frances blushed but then smiled really big, "Well, they sure are pretty."

"Thank you, Miss Frances. My mom will be tickled to hear that." Frances waved and ran back to the group.

"You sure made her day," Florence glanced at Riley, "For a minute there, I wasn't sure they were real myself."

Riley had moved closer to Florence to watch the group of kids finish up with the lassos and turned his head towards her, "What do you think now?" asked Riley.

Florence moved her gaze to the kids and said, "I'll take your word for it."

Chapter 4

Florence opened her eyes, rolled over in her bed, and looked at the clock. It was 7:30 on Saturday morning. She stretched and realized she had two glorious days off. She thought about her first week at her new job. She had seen a lot of the park and was fascinated by what she saw. Lots of rides, a steamboat, a train, a water ride, and best of all, TreeHouse City. That was her favorite. She'd have to ask Ms. McGregor if employees could rent a weekend in a treehouse. She could even invite her sister to stay with her. The only elusive thing had been meeting the boss,

Mr. Simmons. She thought she would have come across him at least once during her first week.

She had met many of the employees in each area of the park and so far, everyone was very welcoming.

One person she couldn't get off her mind was Riley. He was handsome and good with the kids. She caught glimpses of him throughout the day and he'd wave at her on his way across the park. He always seemed to be everywhere, but she hadn't seen him in costume again. Maybe he had two jobs in the park. Maybe one day she'd get up the courage to ask. For some reason, he made her nervous. A good kind of nervous, but nervous, nonetheless.

She couldn't go down that path. Her first real relationship had ended in a tragedy and she just couldn't take the chance to go through that again. She hadn't thought about Keith in a while. She still talked to his sister and his mother. His sister, Leslie, had been a classmate of hers at the University of South Alabama. Keith had just finished at Auburn with an Agribusiness degree, and he was going to be a farmer. He told her that had always been the plan since he was knee high. Of course, it wasn't surprising, seeing how his family had one of the biggest farms in Baldwin County.

When they had first started dating, she had been inundated seeing cattle, corn, cotton, and chickens. You name it, the Dalton family had grown or raised it. She thought Keith was the most handsome man she had ever seen. She always thought he looked like a young Kevin Bacon. She had loved Keith and when he asked her to marry him, her love for him deepened. She was ready to give herself to him completely, but he said they would be married soon enough and he wanted that first night to be special for her. Of course, that didn't stop them from many "almost" first times.

Growing up around farm life, he wasn't squeamish at all in talking about sex. He told her one time as they were cuddled together something his father had said that had made a big impression on him. His father had given him the "talk" when he was young. He told Keith that these were different times. Keith could do what was right for him, but to always respect and protect his partner. Keith had shared with her that he didn't understand until he was in college that his parents exclusively dated each other, and his mom had shared in one of their talks that his parents had waited for each other. Keith's parents had a special marriage.

Florence then thought about Keith's brother. She hadn't

talked to Curtis in a while. He was five years older than Keith. Florence always liked him. He was the big brother she never had. Curtis checked in every so often, usually around the anniversary of Keith's death to see how she was doing. Keith had been coming home from an Agriculture conference when he was hit by a drunk driver. Of course, the drunk driver survived without a scratch. Keith hadn't been that fortunate. He died on impact. Florence felt so lost without him. His family was devastated. They were good about continuing to include her in family gatherings. Of course, they understood why she couldn't go back to the farm. It was just too painful.

Florence took a deep breath, turned back to the clock that read 8:00. It was time to get moving if she wanted to see her sister.

Florence made it to the local coffee shop where her sister worked in record time. The Good to the Last Drop Coffee Shop had a sizable crowd when Florence entered.

Her sister Karen made eye contact with her and nodded as she handed a well-dressed older woman two cups of coffee to go, "Thank you, Mrs. Jenkins and tell Mr. Jenkins I said hello. I hope he feels better soon," said Karen.

"Oh honey, you are the sweetest thing. This King Cake coffee will be just the ticket. You know how Mr. Jenkins likes anything related to Mardi Gras. Bye now!"

Florence took a seat and waited for her sister. Karen was striking in her own way. She reminded Florence of Audrey Hepburn. Diminutive in size and stature, but with a classic look about her, with her long brown hair worn up in a bun. Those classic features sent many male looks her sister's way. Karen had her share of dates, but never got serious about any of them. She was too wrapped up in her studies.

Florence watched the line get smaller. Karen usually got a break about 9:00. She watched her sister serve the last of the customers, and another barista took her spot so she could go on break. Karen brought over two cups and sat next to Florence.

Florence took a sip of the cup in front of her and just sighed. Cafe au lait. Her favorite. She learned to acquire a taste for it during a teacher conference in New Orleans. Of course, the beignets served with the coffee were fabulous as well.

She turned her attention to her sister. Florence said, "Thanks sis. You just made my morning."

"No problem Flo." Florence looked at Karen. Karen was the only one that she allowed to call her that. She didn't know why.

Florence had tried to protect her sister the best she could from their abusive uncle when they were children. Karen had been her saving grace when Keith had died. Karen always had a sweet nature about her. She had been what her crazy uncle had deemed the "runt" of the family and would take any chance to demean and belittle her. Florence was glad to see Karen had gained a little more weight and had gotten taller over the years. Her sister was still too thin for her liking, but she looked happy.

Karen asked Florence if she had talked to their mom, "Yes, last night. We talked for about an hour. She sounded good and said her work had picked up at the office." Their mother, Janet, was a secretary at a local insurance office.

"How's Edward?" asked Florence. Edward Howard was their mom's neighbor, a retired cop who helped put their abusive uncle away. Edward had been crazy about their mom for years. Her mom loved Edward, but didn't want to marry again, even though he had asked. Both sisters believed it had something to do with their dad drinking himself to death and putting them in the position of having to move in with their crazy uncle.

Mom just couldn't trust the fact that a man could love and take care of her, even though Edward tried to change her mind many times. They saw each other all the time, but never made anything official.

"Ed is good, "said Karen. She had a way of shortening names and no one ever seemed to mind. Karen asked, "What does your day look like?"

"Well, I'm as free as a bird this weekend. Of course, I might work on some lesson plans tomorrow. Sunday is always a good day to work on lesson plans."

"Lesson plans are the bane of any teacher's existence. Don't you want to get out and do something fun besides planning all the time?"

"So says the girl who is constantly studying when not working." "Touché," chuckled Karen.

"Tell me about the new job," Karen said, as she stirred sweetener in her coffee.

Florence began to tell her sister all about the park, "I've met so many nice people, and they've been very welcoming."

"How's your new boss?" asked Karen.

"Haven't met him yet," Florence said as she sipped her coffee. "Really, so who hired you?"

"That would be Ms. McGregor. Nice lady and a hard worker." "Meet anyone interesting?" Karen asked.

Florence got quiet and wondered if she should say anything After a minute she said, "Well, I met this guy. His name is Riley and he's a clown at the park, at least I think he's a clown. It's kind of confusing. I saw him at my interview dressed as a clown, but then I'd see him across the park without a clown costume. I was thinking he might have more than one role there."

"Is he cute?" Karen asked. Florence just looked at her and didn't answer.

"Listen Flo, I know Keith is probably going to always be the great love of your life, but he's been gone for 3 years now. It's okay if you start having feelings for another man. You're almost 30."

Florence raised her eyebrows at her sister, "Hey, I'm not there yet."

Karen squeezed her sister's hand," Anyway, what I am saying Flo, is that it's okay."

"Look, I know where you're going with this, but I've finally gotten to the point where I'm feeling settled. I can help you and mom, and I feel really good about that."

"Flo, more than anyone, I appreciate everything you have done for us. I really do.

But I want more for you. I want you to have a life, a real life with someone special who loves you and will take care of you and give you some fun in your life. You deserve it more than anyone."

Florence stared at her sister and couldn't be prouder, "How'd you get to be so wise? I'm supposed to be older and smarter."

Karen grinned, "It doesn't always work that way."

"How well I know, how well I know," Florence agreed as they clinked coffee cups together

Chapter 5

Another Monday dawned bright and beautiful leaving the Sunday rain behind.

Riley caught a glimpse of Florence hurrying into the employee building. He was up top on a high ladder replacing a lightbulb so he couldn't stop what he was doing.

He really needed to come clean and introduce himself properly. He didn't know why he hadn't taken the time to do just that. Maybe it had something to do with someone talking to him as if he wasn't the boss. Once Florence realized who he was, would she become even more the professional? He kept working on the lightbulb and thought about the glimpses of humor he had caught from her, a grin or smile every so often, mostly directed at the children.

Who was he kidding? He wanted more of that directed at him and he knew it was a bad idea. For some reason, he liked her. He also thought he had caught some sadness there when she thought no one was watching. He began looking for her when he was making his rounds through the park. This was also a bad sign.

Maybe it was time to ask someone out. He hadn't seen anyone for quite some time. The dates he had left him bored. The women he dated were nice enough, he guessed. Mostly daughters of his mom's friends. But once they found out that he couldn't spend whole weekends with them, they looked elsewhere. Most women didn't want a man who had a mistress, and the park surely was his mistress for now.

He was finished with the light fixture and called down to Fred, "Coming down!"

Fred signaled that he was ready. Once on the ground, Riley helped Fred store the equipment on the maintenance truck and thanked him.

Riley started off his rounds for the day. About 9 AM he heard something come across his work radio he kept in his pocket, "Mr. Simmons, please report to the Midnight Coaster immediately. Repeat, please report to the Midnight Coaster immediately."

Toni pulled up in the golf cart and gestured for him to get in. "Medic called for?" Riley asked.

Toni replied, "Already put the call in." "Update?" Riley asked.

Toni said, "Coaster at a standstill on the tracks. Pretty upset boy in the car. Florence is with him."

As they pulled up to the Over the Moon Pavilion, they quickly moved into the emergency entrance. The Midnight Coaster was a roller coaster that ran mostly in the dark. There were spotlights scattered here and there to resemble planets and star shaped lights fixed to the ceiling.

Every so often a car stopped on the tracks and the lights were turned on.

Riley called into the radio, "House lights on!" The Midnight Coaster crew flipped the switches and the tracks were then visible along with the coaster. There were other people in the cars, but they were quiet, probably because they weren't sure what was going on in the car with the little boy yelling.

Riley could hear a child's uncontrollable sobbing and yelling, "Get me down, get me down!"

As he quickly climbed the stairs that ran along the coaster, he saw a child in the car with Florence. She was trying to soothe the hysterical 7-year-old. She was asking him to breathe and count. He was having none of it.

"Jason, look at me and breathe. Count with me. One, two, three." He turned his face to hers. "Look at me, one, two three." He was breathing heavily.

As Riley reached the car, he looked at Florence, "Hey, what can I do?" She held up her hand for him to wait, "Jason, ready, one, two, three."

Jason finally looked at Florence and repeated, "One, two, three," He let out a breath.

Florence said, "Again, one, two, three." He repeated, "One, two, three." He let out another breath. Riley waited. Florence said, "One more time. One, two, three, breathe."

Jason pushed out a breath and said, "One, two, three" and then he was calm. Florence said, "Jason, this is Mr. Riley. He is a clown here, among other things."

Riley gave her a quick look, "Well, I see you all over the park, and I'm not sure what your other job is." Riley chose not to respond.

Riley looked at the boy, "Hey Jason, how are you feeling?"

Jason looked up and said, "I'm okay. I thought this was going to be a fun ride, but it was dark, and I don't like the dark and then the car stopped, and we are up kind of high." Riley noticed he was squeezing Florence's hand.

"Well buddy," Riley said," if you look around, it's kind of cool to see what the tracks look like when it's all lit up."

Jason cautiously leaned forward and saw the tracks that ran around the room and up and down, "I guess it's kind of cool."

"See, when people come in here, they never see what it's like with the lights on. You're like a VIP!"

Jason said, "I know what that is! A very important person! Did you hear that Miss Smith?

I'm a VIP!" Florence looked at Riley and smiled. Riley held that gaze and couldn't look away. One of the crew had followed Riley up the steps and asked, "Everything okay up here Mr. Simmons?"

Toni had been right behind the crew member and she stopped dead in her tracks, "Uh oh," she thought. Florence froze.

Riley continued to look her in the eyes and said, "I hope so." Florence looked away and Riley turned to the crew member, "Yes, everything is fine. Jason, there's another two tracks to go over until the coaster gets to the end. Do you want to keep going or do you want to walk down the steps with Ms. McGregor here? She's my right-hand man and a very nice lady."

Jason looked at Riley and said, "I think I'll walk down with the nice lady and then can I call my mom?"

Toni said, "Absolutely! I think I may have a snack down there for you."

As he started to walk down the steps, Jason turned back to Riley, "Um, Mr. Riley, can you ride with Ms. Smith?" He looked at Florence and explained, "I don't want you going alone, you might be scared like I was."

Florence looked from Riley to Jason, "You got it, Jason. That's smart thinking on your part. Thank you."

Riley watched Toni take Jason all the way down the steps and once they were clear, he signaled for lights out and settled in the car next to Florence. An announcer came on the intercom and said, "Okay everyone, you're almost home. Please remember to keep your hands in the cars and here we go." The cars started moving on the track.

"So," Florence said and looked at Riley testily, "Mr. Simmons huh? Nice to meet you sir, finally. Now I get why you were all over the park without the clown costume." Florence folded her arms and looked forward towards the track.

Riley knew an angry woman when he saw one, "Look."

"No, you look, I may get fired for saying this, but did you ever think, Mr. Simmons, to tell me who you were or were you just having a laugh at my expense? Is this some type of joke to play on the new girl? Maybe, instead of firing me I should quit, but I need this job. Come to think of it, I'm not a quitter. I hate deceit, but since you're the boss I can't do much about it, can I?"

"You 'bout done?" Riley asked. That got him an even dirtier look, "Okay, I'll apologize, Florence."

"Miss Smith if you please."

Riley sighed, "Miss Smith, I'm sorry. I can't really explain to you why I didn't come clean right away. Maybe it has to do with the fact that it was nice to have a conversation with you seeing me as Riley and not Mr. Simmons. It felt normal and I feel relaxed when I'm around you." That got him a puzzled look from Florence. Florence looked at Riley as the coaster rolled into the station. Damn, Frances was right, he had the prettiest blue eyes.

As the coaster came to a stop and the seatbelts were unfastened, Riley took her hand to help Florence out of the car,

"All I'm saying is that you have a way of engaging with people and not many can pull that off."

Florence was still looking everywhere but at Riley. "Miss Smith repeat after me, one, two, three, now breathe. Do it again, one, two, three breathe."

Years of teaching had taught Florence how to keep a straight face no matter what shenanigans her class was up to, but she didn't think that would help her now. Florence looked at Riley's blue eyes and saw they were sparkling. Riley looked at Florence and saw that the corners of her beautiful green eyes had begun to crinkle. He began to chuckle. She began to giggle.

Soon, they were both laughing out loud. Riley led Florence to a park bench so they could sit and recover from their laughter.

"Look, Florence, I like you. I think you've done a great job with these kids since you've been here. You've brought the program up a notch and I appreciate that in my employees."

Florence looked around expecting to see the other kids in her group, "Where are my kids?"

"I told Toni to have Professor Poindexter take them to the Science Lab." Florence raised her eyebrows, "Dexy for short. She used to work for Apple, and I coaxed her out of retirement."
"Well, I hope she got the better end of the deal."

That got a grin from Riley.

"Wait, what happened to Jason?"

"Toni texted me. He got to call his mom, got an ice cream bar and happily rejoined his group. "

"Miss Smith, have you managed to see all of the park? You've got an hour until you have to pick up your cherubs. Care to join me for a tour? I need to do my rounds." He also wanted to be close to her for a little while longer. Florence didn't answer right away. Riley waited.

Finally, she said, “Sure, why not.”

They started walking and Florence asked, “Your rounds?”

Yes,” Riley said, “It’s something my father and uncle did every morning, off and on during the day and every night. Helps me make sure everything is okay.”

“Sounds like taking care of a baby.”

“That’s how I see the park, as my baby.”

“Do your dad and uncle still run the park with you?”

Riley swallowed hard and stopped. Florence touched his arm and said, “Did I say something wrong?” Riley looked down at her hand on his arm and lost his train of thought.

Riley cleared his throat. “No, it’s just that my father died when I was 10 and my uncle just passed in March.”

“Oh, I’m so sorry.” She looked into those blue eyes and stood very still.

He caught himself leaning towards her ever so slightly, but Florence let go of his arm and took a step back. They both looked at each other and felt something shift between them.

Riley stepped back and heard himself say, “I appreciate that. Sometimes I feel they still walk the park with me.”

They continued on the tour passing several areas of the park as Riley described each one as they walked: the Sunshine and the Sea area which contained mostly water rides, the Rock and Roll area which had a couple of roller coasters, rock climbing walls, and obstacle courses, and the Storybook and Sweet pea section which housed all of the rides for the little ones and boasted a library. They were rounding the Founding Farmers section when Florence suddenly stopped.

She could see it was set up with tractor displays, old farm equipment with farmers who had been hired to describe the displays and answer any questions for visitors. There were a few farm to table restaurants, a farmer's market, and a barn visitors could walk through. There was even a playground for children set up with rubber tire swings, toy trucks and tractors. There was a field made of AstroTurf with plastic crops they could farm and a pretend grocery store where the kids could weigh their produce and cash out their purchases on an antique cash register. It was truly a homage to the farmers and farms in the area.

Florence didn't realize until Riley touched her arm that tears were rolling down her face. Riley gently said, "Florence?"

Oh, she never thought seeing a farm, even a pretend one, could hit her like this. All she could think about was that Keith never got to live out his dream of farming and building a life. Florence looked up at Riley with tears still in her eyes, "Riley, it's wonderful. It truly is. What a tribute to the farmers. I can't explain it right now," she said to him as she covered his hand, "but thank you."

Riley didn't know what to say. He didn't think she would welcome a hug, so he just held her hand for now. Florence wiped her face, cleared her throat and looked at her watch.

She released her hand from Riley's and stepped away, "Well, I should be getting back.

Thank you for the tour." Riley watched her walk away, frustrated he couldn't do more. His only thought was that he hoped one day she would trust him with the rest of her story.

Florence followed the sidewalk back to the Science Lab to collect her group.

She took a deep breath. She wished she hadn't cried in front of her boss, but seeing the farm was such a shock and the memories of Keith just came flooding back.

Florence collected herself and her group to finish out the day.

When Florence got home, she called her sister. Karen answered on the first ring. “Hey sis. Do you have plans tonight?”

“No,” Karen replied, “What did you have in mind?”

“A pitcher of margaritas? That sound tempting? It’s been one heck of a day!” Karen said, “Yes, I’ll pick you up shortly. Mexican restaurant in Fairhope?” Florence let out a laugh, “I’ll be waiting!”

Back in the office, Riley made his own call to his pal Hunt. “Dr. Huntington here. Oh, it’s you Riley, what’s up?”

“You about done for the day?”

“Yep, just treated my last sore throat. What'd you have in mind?” Riley asked, “What about Mexican?”

“Yeah, sounds good,” Hunt replied, “I should be ready to go in an hour. See you then.”

Chapter 6

As Florence and Karen walked into their favorite Mexican restaurant, they saw it was packed.

"Wow," Florence said, "Crowded for a Monday night!" "Yeah," Karen remarked, "It's summer, remember?"

As they followed the waiter to their table, they passed about a dozen women all laughing, carrying on and passing presents around the table.

There was an attractive woman seated in the middle of the group wearing a sash and a crown with the number "30" blinking on the front of the crown.

Karen looked at Florence. "Birthday party?"

Florence glanced her way and replied, "No, they're teachers." Karen asked, "How do you know they're teachers?"

"I just know. We tend to travel in packs."

Karen looked at the table again and said to her sister, "They look so happy and rested."

Florence sat in her chair, "That means they're retired." Karen looked back at her sister and burst out laughing. As Florence looked at her menu she smiled.

After the waiter delivered a pitcher of margaritas and a

basket of chips, the sisters munched on chips and filled their glasses with the yellowish green concoction.

Florence took a sip, “I needed that.”

“So,” Karen said. “To what do I owe the pleasure of a night out with my sister?”

Florence told Karen about her day with one of the kiddos in her group having a meltdown, “I also found out that Riley and my boss are one and the same.”

Karen asked, “How did you deal with that?”

“I tried to get my anger and frustration across to Riley without getting fired. It didn’t help when I broke down at the farm area.”

Karen held her hand, “Oh, Flo. Keith will always be a part of you. You know that.

His memories will always be there. He was a great guy and loved you with all his heart. Not many people find what you had. It sounds like the park has done a great job honoring him and the farming community.”

Florence felt the tears sting her eyes. She knew her sister was right. She hadn’t expected it to hit her so hard. They talked for a little longer. Florence could always count on her sister to be her sounding board.

After their conversation, the sisters were still perusing the menu when Karen gave a slight whistle and said, “Don’t look now, but a hottie just walked in. Oh, wait, make that two hotties.”

Since Karen was still staring, Florence turned in her chair and couldn’t believe her eyes. Standing at the front of the restaurant was none other than Riley Simmons.

He and another man were following the waiter, when a pretty silver haired lady from the teacher group stopped Riley and asked him to take their picture. Florence watched as Riley flashed a grin and proceeded to take about a half dozen pictures. The ladies then surrounded Riley and his friend. They gave the guys hugs and thanked them both profusely.

As the men grinned and followed the waiter, Florence saw Riley look their way and stop.

He said something to the waiter and motioned his friend to follow. Riley approached Florence and said, "Hello Miss Smith."

Karen raised her eyebrows at the formality. "Mr. Simmons."

Riley said," This is my friend Hunt. Hunt, this is Florence Smith and ..."

Karen spoke up, "Hi, I'm Karen, Flo's sister. Would you gentlemen like to join us?"

Before Riley had a chance to respond, Hunt answered for them both, "That would be great!" Riley looked at Florence and she shrugged.

After both men were seated and ordered drinks, Florence explained to Karen, "This is Mr. Simmons, my boss at the park."

Riley said to Karen, "Riley please. Mr. Simmons seems a little formal since we aren't at work." He swung his gaze to Florence. Riley and Florence stared at each other.

Karen noticed Hunt's mischievous grin. She leaned over his way and whispered, "Am I missing something?"

He looked at her with sparkling eyes and whispered back, "No I think we're just in time for the show."

About thirty minutes later, when all of the chips, tacos, and burritos had been cleared, Florence and Riley watched as Karen and Hunt were swept up in a conga line around the restaurant with the teacher group in the middle of it all. The retiring teacher was leading the line. Florence watched as one lady from the teacher group, a short haired blonde, join the mariachi band, shaking the maracas, with several of the others following her.

Florence smiled at the group as they continued around the room, with Karen and Hunt in tow.

Riley watched the group as well. He shook his head and grinned as he watched his best friend make his way around the restaurant, "You can always pick out a group of teachers, can't you? They're always together and seem to have a lot of fun."

"That's true." Florence agreed. As Florence took a sip of her margarita, she felt Riley's gaze on her.

"Your sister is nice. You two seem close."

"We are."

"Your parents in the area?"

"Mom lives in Mobile. How about yours?"

"She lives in Pensacola, so not too far from the park. I talk to her just about every day." "I keep up with mine too," said Florence.

"And your father?" Riley asked.

Florence was quiet and before Riley could change the subject, she told him her father had died when they were young. Riley apologized and she said, "We didn't know him well. He drank himself to death years ago."

Riley grimaced, "That must have been very hard for all of you."

"Yes, but we survived," Florence offered, "I was able to get a grant to finish college the first time and worked two jobs to get my master's degree. Karen was able to get a partial grant and with both of us working, she will finish her degree and hopefully be on her way to a good job."

Riley was impressed but felt bad for her at the same time, "So, you're taking care of your mom and sister? You seem to be kind of young to do all that. Sounds like you haven't had too much of a break."

"Well," Florence said, "that's how it's been for us and we managed to make it work.

Mom got a job at an insurance agency and does okay." "Sounds like your mom never remarried?"

Florence replied, "She could never trust anyone after her first marriage. The situation we found ourselves in after my father's death wasn't good." Riley wanted to ask, but Florence didn't elaborate and he decided not to push.

They both fell silent.

Riley was the first to break the silence, "Are we good," he paused for effect, "Flo?" "That would be Florence to you, Mr. Simmons."

"So," Riley said, "why don't we start over?" He stuck out his hand, "Hi, I'm Riley Simmons, your new boss".

Florence looked at those beautiful blue eyes and sighed. She shook his hand, "Hi, I'm Florence Smith, your talented new educator."

He grinned and held her hand for a beat longer than necessary. She smiled.

"Wow, Miss Smith, was that smile directed at me? You should do it more often." "I only smile on special occasions," Florence informed him.

Riley shot back with, “Is this a special occasion?”

Florence looked around the room as the conga line started to break up and back at Riley, who was still holding her hand. Before she could answer, Karen and Hunt returned to their seats out of breath and laughing. Karen raised her eyebrows as Florence let go of Riley’s hand. Karen figured she’d get that story later.

Hunt said, “Well, you two, certainly missed out on a good time!” He hit Riley’s arm, “Man, you’re the dancer, you should have been up there!”

Florence and Karen stopped sipping their margaritas and looked at Riley.

They said at the same time, “You’re a dancer?” They grinned at each other.

Riley smiled and when he said nothing, Hunt continued, “Oh, he sings too. He makes the angels weep with that voice of his.”

Florence smiled, leaned forward and said, “Really?”

“My Aunt Alice was hired on by my Uncle Frank as a dancer at the park back in the day. That’s how she and my Uncle Frank met. He said she was the prettiest lady and man, oh, man, could she dance!”

Karen asked, “How did your Uncle get around that with her working for him? I mean, boss and employee dating? That would be a hot topic today.”

“Well,” Riley explained, “He told me that Aunt Alice put him off for a year. She didn’t want anything to look improper. So, he waited. She actually was the one who acted on her feelings first. My uncle told me the two of them were taking a test run on the Ferris wheel after the park had closed for the night and she leaned over and kissed him."

Karen exclaimed, "Awe, that's so romantic! What a story!" Florence asked, "So no one made snide comments?"

Riley took a sip of his beer then replied, "No. The employees were thrilled. They'd been watching their cat and mouse game for a year and were just glad it happened. Aunt Alice was so touched by how she was treated."

Florence spoke up, "Sounds like a happy ending."

Hunt offered, "One of the old timers told me that the employees had a pool going about when and where it would happen. But no one picked the square marked July 21 on the ferris wheel, so they just took all of the money collected and bought a wedding gift they knew they were going to need anyway."

Florence said, "Riley, I'm sorry about your Uncle Frank. Where's your Aunt Alice now?" "She lives in one of our bungalows on the park property. You'll see her from time to time at the park. Hunt and I check on her every day. Even at her age, she's a force to be reckoned with."

Hunt leaned his elbows on the table and sighed, "I love Aunt Alice. I was over at their place so much because Riley and I were thick as thieves, in and out of her house. She would give me cookies and try to teach me how to dance. I never could get the dance moves quite down."

He looked at Riley, "Not like my man Riley did." Hunt sighed again. "Yeah, I actually asked Aunt Alice to marry me once." He and Riley laughed, "Do you remember that Riley?"

Riley's eyes twinkled. Hunt continued, "I had finished med school and we all went out to celebrate. Aunt Alice wanted to go dancing and got me to waltz with her. I was terrible. But she just kept going, ignoring my two left feet. That's when I asked her to marry me."

Hunt looked at Riley and just laughed.

Karen asked, "Well, what was her answer?"

Hunt said, "She told me I was too old for her." They all died laughing.

Riley quipped, "What a smart woman!" This brought up another round of laughter.

Hunt looked at Riley, "We should make plans to bring her out one night and take her dancing." Hunt looked at the sisters. "Say, would you ladies like to join us for a night out with Aunt Alice? Do you dance? It's a requirement. If Aunt Alice is around, there's going to be dancing."

The sisters looked at each other and Karen answered, "We both took lessons growing up. There was a very kind lady at the community center who took us under her wing with all kinds of dance lessons." Karen pointed her finger at Florence, "Now I may be good, but Flo is phenomenal."

It was Riley's turn to lean across the table, raise his eyebrows and say, "Really?" Florence looked down, "Those lessons were a long time ago."

Karen swatted Flo's arm, "Come on Flo, you know you keep up with your workouts and dance moves."

Riley looked at Florence, "Maybe you can fill in sometime if we're down a dancer at the park. We could make sure it doesn't interfere with your groups."

Before Florence could reply, the waiter showed up with the checks.

"Well," Hunt sighed, "This certainly has been a fun night,

but the sun comes up earlier than I'd like."

Everyone paid their tab and gathered their things.

As they passed the empty table where the teacher group had been, they noticed bits of wrapping paper, empty glasses and plates of leftover retirement cake.

Hunt said, "Looks like a good time was had by all." He looked at Florence and said, "You teachers are something else."

Florence just smiled.

Jerry Smith was out in the exercise yard of the jail. He had bartered a cigarette from one of the inmates. There wasn't supposed to be smoking here, but what were they going to do to him? Couldn't be any worse off than where he was now. He kept his head down so the guards wouldn't bother him.

He was watching the other inmates in the yard and thinking of his plan. He had made a few connections while in jail that might help him. He planned to check out the old neighborhood when he got out. He was up for parole in about a month and was going to collect what was his. No one knew about the bag of money he had stashed in the ceiling of his old house. That was going to be his ticket to the big time. He understood that the sniveling sister-in-law still lived there. "That house rightly belongs to me." He'd have to get his friends to "borrow a car" for him.

When he was arrested, the damned judge let her keep the house. He finished the last drag of his cigarette, threw it to the ground and crushed it under his shoe.

He was going to get payback one way or the other. If that brat Florence ruined things for him again, he'd find a way to take her down, right along with anyone else that got in his way.

Chapter 7

Early one Saturday morning, Florence found herself at the fitness studio at the park. She learned that employees were allowed to use the gym for workouts at no cost. She wanted to work out early as she was helping with the cub scout group. Florence normally didn't work on the weekends, but Riley asked if she wanted to help the little boys with activities in the education building.

She opened the doors to the building and saw it was deserted. She could work out to her heart's content. It was a big place. On one side of the building was the gym with weights, ellipticals, treadmills and a juice bar which was closed at the moment. She saw a door connected to the gym and decided to explore. As she walked into the room, she noticed a huge dance floor. She looked around and saw a state-of-the-art sound system. There was a wall-length mirror in the front of the room with barre's attached. Looking up, Florence saw a balcony that ran all the way around the top of the dance studio.

She was curious so she walked up the steps to the balcony and discovered a track. She could come up here after her workout to walk and stretch out. Wow! It was a far cry from the little room in the community center in the neighborhood where she and her sister learned to dance. Florence looked downstairs at the dance floor and since no one was in the building, she thought she'd try out an old dance routine from the community center. She ran down the steps and as she began to stretch, she thought about her job at the park. She couldn't believe it had been a month already. She was beginning to have a love affair with the park. Exploring the park, she always found something new. Every group was different and challenging at times as well. But she really enjoyed being here.

As she finished her last stretch, she programmed in Walter Murphy's A Fifth of Beethoven from 1977. Her teacher at the center had a thing for songs from the 70's and this was Florence's favorite. Florence faced the back wall because she wasn't quite ready to dance in front of the mirror.

As the music started, Florence turned in a circle around the middle of the dance floor.

Jazz steps came first with Florence following the music with turns, grand jetes and jumps. She pumped her shoulders and moved forward, letting the music take over and move her around the room.

Riley let himself into the gym and walked up the back steps to the track. His team members were opening the park this morning and since it was still early, he thought he'd get in a run. He heard the music in the studio and looked over the balcony. He couldn't believe his eyes. It was Florence dancing. He'd never seen anyone move that fast and that fluidly. She changed from jazz to hip-hop to ballet to disco and worked the dance floor like no one's business.

He crept quietly to the top of the steps and took a seat.

He was mesmerized. Riley watched her spin, glide and move her hips and that was not even the best part. As the music came to a crescendo, she performed pirouette after pirouette. She did ten in a row! This was amazing!

As the music was ending, she slid on her knees towards the center of the room, stopped and held her hand up high. She was stunning. He bet his heart was beating faster than hers and he was just sitting. He must have made a slight movement because Florence looked up towards the stairs.

She stood up, surprised, "Oh. I thought I was alone."

Riley stood up. He clapped and whistled as he came down the steps wearing a Van Halen t-shirt, a pair of Under Armour shorts and his beloved pair of beat up Nike shoes.

Florence smiled as she bent down to get her towel out of her gym bag. She said, "I didn't think anyone would mind if I used the dance floor."

Riley replied, "I didn't mind at all!" and they laughed comfortably.

He asked, "You learned all that at the community center you talked about?"

"Yeah, pretty much. The teacher was a good instructor. Plus, when I was in college, some of the girls and I would go out and dance, which kept me up on the latest dances. Since I love 70's music, the DJ was good enough to humor me and played a 70's list."

Riley said, "I'm impressed."

"So," Florence asked, as she bent down to stretch, "When do I get to see your moves?" Riley raised his eyebrows, grinned and rocked back on his feet.

"Dance moves...you know what I meant," Florence rolled her eyes as she sat on the floor to stretch, shaking her head and muttering something about men.

"I'm not sure I do, might need some examples," Riley chuckled.

"I am shutting down this conversation," Florence smiled, "it's going nowhere." Riley laughed, "You sure about that?"

Florence looked up and gave him a stern look, "Yeah, I'm pretty sure."

Florence finished with her stretches, and she started to stand. Riley moved at the same time. They collided and Riley reached out both arms to steady her. Florence held on to his arms. Neither moved as they took a deep breath. Riley stepped forward. Both jumped as they heard a door slam in the next room. They stepped back and let go of each other.

An early morning yoga class streamed into the room. The instructor noticed Riley and waved. He waved back.

"Well," Florence said, "That's my cue. See you later." She exited the studio.

Riley put in his ear buds, walked up the stairs to the track and thought to himself, "Sure hope I'll be seeing you later. Sure hope so."

That afternoon, a steady rain greeted the guests at the park.

There were full houses in the arcades, the restaurants, and the inside venues.

Riley, dressed in official park rain gear, drove his golf cart around to check on any situations that would come with the weather. He had a handful of his staff doing the same.

He loved living in Alabama. If you ever ask a native Alabamian about the weather, the response would be, "We get all four seasons. They just all happen at one time in the same month." His favorite was, "If you don't like the weather in Alabama, just wait a minute." Riley chuckled to himself.

The heat, the rain, hurricanes, tornadoes.... he had seen it all. It was top priority to see to the safety of his guests and employees. He had daily weather updates and weekly drills.

He had checked with all his ride captains for them to be mindful of safety rules in case of dangerous thunderstorms and lightning. So far, the forecast called for a steady rain which should be out of the area by 4PM. He had checked on all his departments as well and that's how he knew Florence was in the Education building teaching her group.

As he drove through the park, his thoughts went back to this morning at the dance studio. If the exercise class hadn't interrupted when they did, he was pretty certain he would have had his first kiss with Florence Smith, which might not be the best idea.

He needed to keep his mind focused on the park and his family. He didn't know if he could afford a relationship at this point in his life. Running the park was a big responsibility that rested on his shoulders. He couldn't afford to make mistakes, as he had many people depending on him for their livelihoods.

He just couldn't seem to get her out of his mind. Florence was in his thoughts when he went to sleep and when he got up first thing in the morning, not to mention when they crossed paths during the day. He was sure his Uncle Frank's words of wisdom would be to follow your heart. If only it were that easy.

Florence listened to the steady patter of rain as the group of ten teenagers waited for her direction. She had the cub scout group to teach after this one. The education building was located in the middle of the park. There were two trails in the back of the building, but due to the steady rain, were not in use currently. Right before she was to start the lesson, the door opened. Riley walked in, nodded to Florence, and took a seat in the back of the room.

She looked back at her group and said, “Ok. We’re going to do an activity about work skills. What that means is I have outlined a situation on each handout I’m about to give you. The activity will focus on job skills and situations you may find yourselves in when getting a job.

You have to work through the situation with a partner.” Groans could be heard around the room. Florence held up a hand, “All right, all right. I have the list of partners written on the board. You can use anything you see in this room to help you figure out the situation. Okay, first group done, come up and ring the bell. Ready? Go!”

As the group dispersed to the front of the room to see the partner list, one of the teenagers stayed in his seat. Florence looked at her attendance roll and headed to the back of the room.

Slouched in his desk was a tall, lanky boy, with blonde hair long enough to be hiding part of his face. He had an earring in each ear, tattered jeans and scuffed up tennis shoes. His name was Kevin Sharp.

“Hey Kevin. Anything I can help you with? The rest of the group is starting the activity and your partner is waiting for you at the front of the room.”

Kevin looked around Florence and saw a big kid who looked like he worked out regularly. He was wearing a muscle t- shirt with the name of a local high school sports team. He was leaning on a table in the front of the room.

“I’ll pass,” Kevin said. Riley shifted in his seat.

Florence took a moment and said, “Well, Kevin, you did sign up to be in here today, right?”

Kevin said, “I didn’t sign up for it. I don’t even want to be here. My dad signed me up because he said I couldn't just stay at home sleeping all day and watching TV. He had to work. Neighbor dropped me off."

Florence looked at Kevin and asked, "So what's the plan here?"

Kevin said, "No plan, just don't want to do whatever it is you got going on here."

At that moment, the teenager named Josh with the muscle shirt walked to the back of the room and stood by Florence, "Hey man, I'd like to get started. Everybody else is working on this project and I'm ready to get going."

Kevin stood up, "Well, that's gonna to be a problem." Florence saw Riley casually stand up and move closer. Josh said to Kevin, "It doesn't have to be a problem."

At that point one of the other teenagers in the group called out to Josh and told him he was welcome to join their group if it was okay with Miss Smith.

Josh looked at Kevin and asked Florence if it would be okay with her if he joined the other group. Florence sighed, "Yes, Josh, that's fine."

Josh gave one more look to Kevin and walked towards the other group. Kevin said to Florence, "And I don't need a lecture either."

Florence replied, "I wasn't about to give you one. Why don't you tell me what you're interested in and what you like to do?"

Kevin shrugged his shoulders and said, "Guess I'd like to make me some money, like anyone would hire me."

Riley leaned against the back wall and listened.

Florence asked, "How are you going to get a job if you don't try?" Kevin shrugged his shoulders, "I don't know."

At that point Riley walked over and joined the conversation, "Miss Smith, mind if I join you?"

Florence looked around as the others were still working on their assignment and said to Riley, "Sure Mr. Simmons. Mr. Simmons, this is Kevin. Kevin, this is Mr. Simmons."

Kevin just looked at Riley and said, "Who are you? I thought she was the teacher," pointing at Florence.

Riley said, "I kind of run this place."

Kevin replied testily, "What are you going to do man, throw me out?"

Riley countered with, "Did you hear me say anything about throwing you out?"

"No, but that's usually what happens to me. I walk into a store in the neighborhood, the owner usually takes one look at me, doesn't like the way I look and points to the door. I've had teachers get an attitude with me because I don't want to talk, and they think I'm being belligerent."

"Belligerent, huh?" asked Florence.

Riley interjected, "What skills do you have?"

Kevin was silent for so long that Florence didn't think he was going to answer.

Riley just waited. Florence took that moment to look over to see how the others were doing in their groups. They were still working.

Kevin took a deep breath and said, "I don't know how I can do this, but I can see what happens next. Like I can predict the outcome of something just by looking at a pattern or sequence of events. Like my dad tried to teach me how to play chess, and

I beat him the first time---never played it before. I can work my way around a computer like nobody's business. I don't know how, I just can."

Riley looked at Kevin and then at Florence. He took a card out of his pocket and handed it to Kevin. Kevin asked, "What's this?"

Riley responded, "With the skills you're describing, I sure could use you in our tech department here. Just so happens I have a student assistant tech spot open.That card has my contact info on it. If you're interested, talk to your dad. If he can take some time off, I can meet with you both here in my office and we can hammer out the details. Pay would be minimum wage, but it would give you a starting point toward making some money at least."

Florence watched Kevin look at the card. At that moment a bell rang at the front of the room, "Well," Florence said, looking at Riley and Kevin, "I'll leave you two to talk while I check out what the group has found. Kevin, once you finish talking to Mr. Simmons here, how about joining the group for the next activity? It's in the computer lab with Professor Poindexter. She rocks. I think you'll find it interesting."

Florence smiled at Kevin, patted Riley's arm and went to join the group at the front of the room. Kevin glanced at Riley and said "Why would you take a chance on me?"

Riley looked at Kevin and replied "You remind me of a friend I knew back in high school. He had talent too, but he got beat down by life and instead of asking for help, made one bad decision after another. His life might have turned out differently if he'd had this opportunity. You have my contact info on that card. Up to you to use it."

Kevin looked down at the card. As Riley walked across the

room to leave, he looked up to see Florence watching him. He gave her a wink and continued on his way.

Chapter 8

Florence arrived at TreeHouse City that afternoon to help with the Cub Scout group. The rain had been replaced by sunshine. She had already met one of the boys on the day she interviewed for her job here. His name was Scott Williams. His father, Jacob, had contacted her after witnessing her interaction with his son. He was impressed that someone could adjust to his learning style so quickly. He told her his son had a diagnosis of Autism and loved being a Cub Scout. Loud noises bothered him. He and Scott had worked out strategies to help him cope in a public environment. Jacob had volunteered to be a Cub Scout leader so he could be assured that his son would have an advocate during these weekend outings. He had done his research and contacted the local agency for Autism. Victoria McGregor was the director of the agency. She would be meeting them here today.

Florence understood that along with being the director of the agency, Victoria was also Toni McGregor's daughter. Florence heard the shouts of children exiting the treehouses. She smiled, ready to be embraced by the energy of first graders. Florence watched the group advance towards her and counted about 10 kids and three adults. Scott made a beeline for her. It was neat how some children never forgot a teacher who showed kindness.

Scott had wispy blonde hair sporting a cowlick on the back of his head, "Hi, I'm Scott. I know you." He patted his earbuds and beamed at Florence.

"Hello, Scott. I'm Miss Smith. How are you today?"

"I'm great! Oh, man, Miss Smith, you should see the TreeHouse we slept in last night. I stayed up all night looking out the window. I could see the moon and everything! My dad said if I didn't go to sleep, I was going to crash today and miss out on all of the fun." Scott took a breath.

The man Scott mentioned appeared behind him and placed his hands on his son's shoulders. "Hi, I'm Jacob Williams." As they shook hands, Florence took in the blonde hair, blue eyes and tan features that matched his son's.

"Nice to meet you Mr. Williams."

"Jacob, please," he responded.

Florence nodded and looked to her left as Toni and a young woman walked up to the group.

"Hi, Florence. I wanted you to meet my daughter, Victoria."

Florence shook Victoria's hand, "It's nice to finally meet you. Toni has told us a lot about you."

"It's Tori, please." She looked at her mom, "I hope it was all good!"

Toni raised her eyebrow. Florence laughed and said, "Yes! She's very proud of you."

Florence thought Tori was the image of Toni with her toned figure and beautiful mahogany skin. Florence inclined her head towards Scott and his father, "Tori, this is Jacob Williams and his son, Scott."

Jacob turned around and his eyes widened, "Ms. Toni? Oh,

my goodness!" He laughed and hugged Toni, "It's been forever!"

Toni laughed and hugged Jacob, "Jacob Williams, I haven't seen you in ages! How are you?"

He nodded at his son, "We're doing okay." Then, Jacob looked at the woman standing next to Toni, "Tori? You're the director of the Autism Center I'm meeting with today? I never put it together." He hugged Tori.

Jacob turned to Florence, "My mom and Ms. Toni were good friends when I was growing up. I used to play with Tori at her house all of the time." He glanced at Tori and she smiled,

"Y'all had a swimming pool. Tori, you and I were like fish, swimming all the time. Do you remember when we were seven years old and exchanged wedding vows in front of your mom's angel statue by the pool?" His eyes filled with laughter, "We decided not to go through with it, so we just jumped back in the pool." He grinned.

"Oh, to be seven again!" Tori groaned.

Scott walked up to his dad. His dad put his arm around Scott. "Scott, this is Ms. Toni and her daughter, Tori."

Tori held out her fist and said, "Hey there, Scott." He looked up at his dad who nodded his head.

Scott grinned and hit Tori's fist with his own.

Tori's heart melted at the sight of his grin with two front teeth missing. Her gaze traveled up to meet Jacob's eyes, which were filled with a sign of relief.

Florence was soon joined by Riley, her boss, "Hi, Florence."

"Riley, how are you?"

His blue eyes met hers, "Great, just thought I'd come over

and say hello to the kids." He saw Tori. "Toni told me you'd be by!" He stepped in her direction to give her a big hug. Her mouth turned up as she hugged him back. Riley turned to the group, "Hi kids! You're in for a treat today with Miss Smith." Florence glanced at him as amusement filled her eyes.

"Y'all be on your best behavior with Miss Smith and have fun!"

Scott was standing near Riley. His eyes widened. Riley squatted down in front of Scott. "Hey, I know you. You're Bongo." Scott had a hard time getting his words out. "Where did the clown go?" Tori handed Riley a key ring of picture cards.

He pulled out the icon card with a man lying in a bed sleeping and showed it to Scott.

"He's sleeping today. Aww, that's no fun. I stayed awake last night and watched the moon out of my window at the TreeHouse. I heard an owl hoot! I heard a frog too! It was loud!"

Riley's eyes filled with laughter, "My best friend, Hunt, and I used to love to stay in those tree houses. We'd stay up all night listening to the animals like crickets and owls. It was fun."

Scott grinned as Riley stood up. He turned to Florence, gave her the key ring of cards and winked.

Florence sighed at those pretty blue eyes and pulled on a train conductor's hat. Riley laughed, "Nice hat."

She smiled, "Just wait for the rest." She turned to the kids and told them to get in line.

The troop leaders guided the cub scouts to the line. Jacob hugged Toni and promised to come see her before they left the park. "Okay, now, let's pretend we're on a train. Everybody raise their foot and step on the train." Florence showed them how to step up and put their foot back down.

"Now we're on a train. I'm Miss Smith, your conductor." She touched her hat, pulled her elbow down and said, "Choo Choo!" She looked at the kids, "Now, you do it. Ready? Choo Choo!" She watched as they pulled their elbows down and yelled, "Choo Choo!"

Riley grinned at Florence. It was her turn to wink at him.

"Follow me and make the Choo!Choo! Sound." The Cub Scout troop followed Florence around the park into the Education building. When she had all the scouts settled in a classroom, she suggested to the adults they could take a break in the teacher's workroom or tour the building. Two of the troop leaders nodded at Jacob. He asked Tori if they could talk in one of the empty classrooms.

She followed him as they made themselves comfortable, "It's good to see you Jacob! It has been a long time." Tori had pamphlets for Jacob, which she handed over to him. "How can I help you today?"

He glanced at Tori. She wasn't what he expected. He hadn't seen her in a long time, but she had grown into a beautiful young woman. Jacob cleared his throat, "I don't know how much you need to know about Scott's background and diagnosis."

"As much as you'd like to tell me or as little. But the more I know, the better I can help you."

Jacob nodded and spoke up, "I'm a Biology professor at USA in Mobile. I try to have a more flexible schedule in the summers and on the weekends. We live in Baldwin County so Scott can access the Special Services programs he needs to be successful in school. He's had great teachers so far. They do a great job transitioning Scott to as many General Education classes as well."

Jacob took a breath, "Is there anything else you'd like to know?" Tori glanced down at her notebook, "Help from family members is very important for Scott to transition from the home to any public environment. It's always good to have support. May I ask you a question?"

"Go ahead," he said.

"Just from the short time I've seen him interacting with you, it seems like Scott relies on you. How does he do in response to mom and how does she interact with him?"

Jacob sat quietly. He sighed and began to speak, "At first we didn't understand how to help Scott. He didn't know how to interact with the other kids on the playground, didn't pick up on social cues, and didn't want to be touched. That was hardest on his mom. She wanted to cuddle and read to him at night. I just wanted to hold my son." Jacob looked away and cleared his throat. Tori laid her hand on top of his. Jacob turned his hand over and squeezed hers before letting it go, "Thank you, Tori." He took a breath, "Okay, let me tell you the rest. His mom is a professor as well, but in Economics. She tried.We went to meetings to help Scott. You know, Early Intervention and Special Services." Tori nodded her head.

"It's not easy being a parent of a special needs child. But, as parents, I believe you need to do everything possible to help your child. I was putting a lot of time into helping our son. She just couldn't do it. Our marriage began to fall apart. We divorced shortly afterwards. She moved to Boston to be closer to her sister. That was about 2 years ago."

Tori glanced at Jacob, "Has she spoken to him since?" Jacob shook his head.

Tori took a breath, "That has to be hard on you. Has he asked about his mom?"

"At first. Then, as time passed, we got into a routine and he stopped asking when his mom was coming home." A tear fell from Jacob's eye. He stood up to look out of the window.

As much as she wanted to give comfort to him, Tori remained seated.

One of the troop leaders knocked on the glass door and signaled to Jacob it was time to go. Tori gathered her notebook and stood up to hand Jacob the packets. As she looked at him, she remembered he had the kindest blue eyes she'd ever seen. Tori handed him the packets and touched his arm, "It's not going to be easy, but I think Scott will have a better life with you in his corner."

"Tori, I won't lie to you. I thought when I talked with you on the phone that you sounded very young to be in this position and couldn't possibly give us what we needed. I didn't recognize your voice since we lost touch over the years. I'm so glad I found out it was you."

He looked at her and waited. She smiled, "I just turned thirty." She waited and glanced back at Jacob.

His mouth turned up, "So did I, but six months ago."

"Well, happy thirtieth."

As they walked towards the door to meet up with his group, he smiled and said, "We'll see." As promised, Jacob and Scott visited with Ms. Toni on their way out of the park. Jacob realized he was disappointed he didn't get to see Tori before she left. Jacob and Scott exited the park, but not before accepting a dinner invitation from Ms. Toni. It sure was good to see her and Tori today. He thought about his meeting with her. Jacob felt she could help him improve Scott's life. He smiled and thought maybe she could improve his life as well. He looked forward to seeing her again.

Jerry Smith was a free man! He didn't know how, but he was free! The parole board approved it that morning. He still had to check in with some damn parole officer, but he'd figure that out when the time came. He found out from a contact that neither the cop nor his niece had shown up to talk to the parole board. Something about the officer who was supposed to contact his niece had retired and someone dropped the ball in letting them know when the meeting was happening. Since there were no objections, the board felt he had served his time.

As he went down to the first floor with two officers to collect his personal belongings, he couldn't stop grinning. He'd lay low for a while and then start his new life, after he took care of eliminating some people from the old one. He had some people in place to help with that too.

As he left the prison, he stopped, raised his arms up to the sky, took a deep breath of fresh air and started walking.

Chapter 9

As the post-Labor Day crowds traveled home and students worked their way back to school campuses, the park settled down with a different crowd. This was the time of year when locals came back out to visit the beaches, restaurants, and theme parks.

Riley made his way through the park's J.F. Simmons Southern Hospitality Center.

This building was a one stop, one shop place with 8 floors that housed all the supplies and equipment for the park. The 1st floor area was the only floor opened to the public. It contained a food court and a gift shop among other things. Riley crossed to the private elevator that only certain trusted staff members could use. He entered the code, stepped in, and pressed the button for the 8th floor. As was his daily routine, he touched the two framed pictures hanging in the elevator and said, "Hello Dad. Hello Uncle Frank." Justin Atticus Simmons and Franklin Delano Simmons stared at him from the back wall of the elevator, bigger than life.

When the building was built, Riley's mother, Mary, suggested to the two men that after all the sweat and tears they put into building the park, there should be something signifying their legacy. So, the J.F. Simmons' name inscribed on the outside of the building honored the two brothers, Justin and Frank. Riley had added the two framed pictures when he graduated high school. He told his Uncle Frank he missed his dad so much but was so grateful he still had him. He wanted to add the pictures so he would be reminded of them every day. As the elevator stopped on the 8th floor, Riley swiped his ID card and the doors opened. As he walked out from the elevator, he scanned his surroundings. Seeing the whole park from this height was a bird's eye view of what was happening. He knew drones could do the same thing he was doing now, but he hated to introduce something into the park that could be considered too intrusive. Of course, he had cameras positioned all around the park for security reasons, but a drone was something different. He just wasn't there yet.

The park was shifting gears from summer to fall. Not summertime crowd numbers, but still a good crowd. The fall and harvest decorations for the park would be going up soon and their yearly Fall Extravaganza Weekend would be coming up in two weeks. This would entail working at night after the park closed to install and hang decorations.

It was usually a crowded, but fun weekend. It was always like a homecoming, seeing family and friends he didn't always have time to see during the rest of the year.

Riley scanned the park again and thought about how hard his dad and uncle worked to make their dream of building a theme park where visitors could come and just have fun Life had become a 24/7 type of world in which people didn't take time for vacations. His dad and uncle hoped to change that or at least give people a place to unwind, smile and get lost in the moment.

He turned away from the railing and walked over to the rooftop garden. Sometimes, at the end of an evening, he would come up here and sit in the quiet. Well, as quiet as it can be for a theme park full of after hour employees. Most nights he could hear the sounds of traffic over on I-10 along with the calling from frogs and crickets and the occasional owl. But as he lowered himself in one of the comfortable chairs in the garden, he gazed at his mother's prized roses.

Somehow his mom managed to grow beautiful pink, yellow and red roses and took care of the garden by herself. He told her he had a grounds crew for that, but his mom said that it gave her something to do after his dad's death and made her feel needed. Riley told her she would always be needed. Mary Simmons told her son that sometimes needs change and people must be ready to change right along with those needs. He couldn't have said it better himself.

Florence and Karen opened the door to the TreeHouse where they would be staying for the weekend, "Flo, this is going to be great!" Karen glanced around at her home for the next two nights.

"I got us the package deal and being an employee, I got a discount. I'm so excited for us," Florence said as she and Karen unpacked a couple of bags of groceries and put their bottles of wine on the kitchen counter, "We get to roam the park, ride on every ride and we get two free meals. What do you want to do first?"

Karen looked at the brochure and map of the park. She eyed the wine and grinned, "How about we start with a glass of wine and go from there?"

Florence laughed and got the wine glasses out she brought with her, "I like the way you think, sis." They sipped their wine and made plans for the evening.

The sisters made their way down from the TreeHouse and

happened to meet Riley making his rounds. His eyes met Florence's, "Ladies, I heard you were staying with us for the weekend. How do you like the TreeHouse?"

Florence eyed Riley, "It's wonderful. We love the layout. Your uncle and dad outdid themselves. You should be proud of what you all have built here."

He smiled fondly, "I am. I miss them tremendously." He looked around him and said, "But I have memories of them everywhere I go here, so it's like they're always with me."

Florence put her hand on his arm. A smile reached Riley's eyes as he put his hand on top of hers. After a minute, she moved her hand and took a breath, "Well, we're heading out to enjoy ourselves. What do you recommend we do first?"

"We actually have dinner and a show tonight in the Wild Wild West section you shouldn't miss. It's a great line up."

Karen replied, "We did see you've got a list of shows and there's a concert tomorrow night. I can't believe you were able to get that singer here. He's very famous and in demand right now."

Riley grinned, "He owed me a favor." He gazed at Florence, who smiled at him. His mouth curved, "You ladies have a good night. Call me if you need anything."

Florence watched Riley walk away and Karen bumped her arm, "What?" asked Florence. "You know what." replied Karen.

Florence grinned and hooked her arm with her sister's, "Let's go to a show!" The two sisters had a great night. The show was energizing, and they rode every ride they could. They bumped into Riley again over at the Midnight Coaster and he took them for a tour behind the scenes. He even took them up to the rooftop garden. Karen went to explore his mother's prized roses as he joined Florence at the railing, "Riley, the view from up here is spectacular. This is where you come to unwind, isn't it?' She looked at him with understanding in her eyes.

He shook his head and met her gaze, "How did you know that?"

"I don't know. Just a guess from what I've come to know about you. You've got a lot of responsibility on your shoulders and just seem to take it in stride." She took a deep breath, "I haven't seen anyone with you, at least not at the park, so you must count on Hunt and your family to talk with and ease the burden. So, it only makes sense you have some place to go to help with the stress. It's beautiful up here."

His gaze never wavered, "No, I'm not seeing anyone. I haven't met anyone over the years who understands my obligations here. It doesn't leave a lot of room or time for dating. I can't just drop what I'm doing and go places on the weekends. It would take a special person to understand my life." Her hand found his and he held on.

Karen called out to Flo to check out the roses. She squeezed his hand and let it go. As the sisters took in their fill of the roses and the garden, Riley asked if they would like to have a tour of all of the floors of the building. They told him they would love that. They had fun exploring each floor. Parade costumes in every shape and color, fun prizes to win at the kids' playing areas and different types of banners and equipment for the park were all there. At the end of the evening, Riley walked the sisters back to the TreeHouse. Karen told Riley goodbye and made her way up the steps.

Florence glanced at him as a slow smile surfaced on his face, "Thank you, Riley, for the tour. We had a nice night." Before she could change her mind, she moved close to him and gave him a hug. Surprise lit up his eyes, but then he held onto her for a minute. They let go of each other with Riley holding on to her hand. His eyes warmed as did hers. She took a step back and dropped her hand, "Goodnight. Sweet dreams, Riley."

"Oh, you can count on it Florence. Goodnight." Riley watched as she climbed the steps to the TreeHouse. Florence turned back, smiled, then went inside. Riley put his hands in his pockets, whistling, as he began to walk back through the park.

Florence woke in the wee hours hearing ringing. She fumbled for the phone and looked at the screen, "Riley, what's the matter? Aunt Alice okay?'

"Yes, she's with my mom in Pensacola. I want you and Karen to get dressed. Hunt just called. I'm taking you all to see your first jubilee! I'll meet you in the parking lot right behind your TreeHouse. You are game, right?"

Florence was now wide awake, "Yes! Give us 10 minutes and we'll be down!" She hung up the phone and shook her sister, "Karen, wake up! We're going to a jubilee! Hurry!"

Karen looked at the excitement on Flo's face and decided to humor her by getting out of bed at three o'clock in the morning.

The sisters met Riley in the parking lot as he jumped out to open their doors, "I packed a cooler just in case for fish and an extra with water." He smiled with enthusiasm, "I've only seen one in my life and it's a very rare occasion.

Karen asked, "So, where are we going?"

Riley replied, "Hunt and his parents are at Father Murphy's bay house. He is an old Irish Catholic priest that he and his family have been friends with for a long time. He has this neat old bay house. Hunt and his parents took me there when we were growing up. Anyway, he has plenty of room in the house, so they decided to stay over with him. They heard someone next door yelling, 'Jubilee!' and that's when he called me."

After about forty-five minutes of driving, Riley pulled into a long shell driveway dotted with big pine trees on either side. In the middle of million-dollar homes which were raised up on pilings, sat an old cinder block house. It was two stories high and had a character all its own. As they rounded the corner of the house, they saw people scattered in the water scrambling to scoop up crabs and shrimp with nets. Others used a gig to get the flounders which surfaced in the water. Riley handed Florence and Karen each a bucket as he carried a gig with him.

They spotted Hunt first who was ankle deep in the water, "Hey, it's about time you all made it! This probably won't last much longer but come see!" They walked down the steps to a small beach and joined Hunt who introduced Karen and Florence to Father Murphy.

The sisters glanced at the older man who looked to be in his 80's with white hair, a tanned face creased with character lines, and eyes as green as the fields of Ireland, "Well, hello lasses. I'm glad you could see the jubilee." He turned to Hunt, "The lad here says this is the first one you've been to, is that right now?"

Karen nodded and said, "Yes, sir."

He winked at her and said, "Lass, just call me Father Jimmy." She smiled, "Yes, Father Jimmy."

"Well, let's get to it. Riley, I see that you're as ready as ever," Father Murphy said as he patted him on the back.

"What's up, Father Murphy?" asked Riley.

"Son, thankfully not my body six feet under looking at dirt on top of me," He grinned and winked at Florence and Karen. Father Murphy's mirth was infectious. As the guys began gigging flounder, the sisters put them in the buckets. Riley showed Florence how to gig a flounder. On her first try, she missed the flounder, lost her balance, and landed on her bottom in the water.

Riley grinned. As he helped her up, she landed in his arms, "Well, Florence, you can stay right where you are or take your chances with the flounder."

She smiled at him as her eyes met his. She took a deep breath and moved from his arms, "I think I should try again."

He winked at her, "Your loss." He showed her once more how to hold the gig, "You have to be patient and then just gig it." He pulled it up and the sharp point had speared a flounder.

He handed over the gig. Florence took her time then got the sharp point through the flounder, "I did it! Look! I got a flounder!" They all clapped for her as she danced around with the flounder on the end of the gig.

Riley teased her, "Okay, Captain Ahab, you need to put the flounder in the bucket, so it won't slip off and ruin all your hard work that went into getting that."

Florence looked around and saw Father Jimmy walking with Karen on the wharf. He showed her how to cast a net to catch shrimp. She flung the net several times only to come up empty, "Let me show you, lass." He cast the net, pulled it up and several shrimp spilled out on the wharf.

Hunt joined them, "Father Murphy, if you strain something and we have to take you to the ER, my parents are going to blame me for not looking out for you."

"Nonsense, lad. I'm fit as a fiddle." He eyed him, "You should know since you did my last check up."

Karen looked at Hunt, "I thought you were a pediatrician."

"Well, lass, when you're an old man like me, this lad here makes an exception." Hunt grinned at Fr. Murphy, "Just want to keep in the good graces of the Lord."

"Don't be cheeky, now, lad." He looked around, "Where are your parents? I saw them earlier." He looked at Karen, "Do you know his parents?"

Karen shook her head, "No, Father Jimmy, we haven't met."

Hunt glanced around, "There they are." His parents were each holding a bucket filled with fish. Oliver and Annie Huntington looked towards the wharf and spied their son with a young lady and Father Murphy. They greeted Riley first and then met Florence. As they made their way onto the wharf, they put their buckets down on the end and then walked over to see their son, "Mom, Dad, this is Karen, Florence's sister."

His mom smiled, "Hello, Karen. We've heard a lot about you and your sister from Hunt and Riley. We understand this is your first jubilee. What do you think so far?"

Karen glanced at the brown haired petite woman dressed in a pair of white pants rolled up to her knees with a faded green camping shirt on top of that and replied, "So far, it's been a lot of fun, except for my lack of being able to catch shrimp with that net Father Jimmy is holding."

"Now you've gone and done it, girl. They won't let me have any fun now. Got my doctor right next to me. He won't let anything happen to me, would you lad?"

Oliver Huntington and his son were the spitting image of each other. Oliver eyed his favorite priest, "Now, Father Jimmy, what are we going to do if you sprain something? Who would say mass at the church we like so much? One of those young men who are just learning to give sermons. What good does that do us?"

"Ollie, one of these days the good Lord is going to see fit that he needs my company, and you would just have to adjust." He patted Hunt's dad on the cheek, "Now, as long as I'm on God's green earth, I'll do as I please." He looked at the man who had been his parishioner and friend for many years. The couple had been inconsolable when they lost their first son at birth but were proud when their second son grew up to be a doctor. The family had nothing at one time, but with perseverance and his help, they thrived. This family had helped him for years by taking care of the church and looking after him. Now, their son, the doctor, took care of him and made sure he had a few more years to look forward to on earth.

Florence and Riley joined the group on the wharf. Florence set down a bucket of crabs.

Father Murphy spied the bucket, "Oh, lass, what a great job there." He leaned down and picked up a crab.

Florence cautioned the priest, "Careful you don't get pinched, Father Jimmy."

"Oh, lass, I've been holding crabs for quite some time now. Here, you just hold the back of them, so they don't have a chance to grab hold of your finger. Try picking one up."

Florence glanced at him, "I'm not sure about that. I like all of my fingers intact."

He waited patiently. She shrugged her shoulders and put her hand behind a crab in the bucket and held it up.

"Well, look at you," Riley declared, "now all you have to do is get used to dropping them in boiling water. Then, you'll have the tastiest crabs you've ever eaten."

She looked at him like he'd lost his mind, "Why would I do that to these poor creatures?

They didn't do anything to me."

He just shook his head, "Stick with me kid and we'll make you a true fisherman yet."

Hunt looked at the group assembled with him and smiled. He was surrounded by good friends and his family. He thought about what his old friend, the Irish priest, said to his father earlier. Thoughts of sadness surrounded his heart. He truly would miss the old guy when he did go to his reward. Father Jimmy caught his eye and put his hand on his shoulder, "Well, lads and lasses, it looks like the party is breaking up. How about I make us a big Irish breakfast and we show young Florence here how to put these crabs' lives to rest?"

The neighbors and friends dotted along the beach all waved to each other and said their goodbyes. The group on the wharf looked around and noticed that the crustaceans and fish were all gone, swept back into the bay. Although rare, there would eventually be another red tide, calm water and the right conditions for another jubilee.

The group surrounding the old priest followed him into his gray cinder block bay house.

The sisters took in the simple decor. To the right was a china cabinet which they learned belonged to Father Jimmy's mother. He had it shipped all the way from Ireland years ago after his mother passed. There was a small living room to the left and a dining room table snuggled not far from the china cabinet. As the girls walked further into the room, they landed in the kitchen. Karen noticed taped to the wall was a sheet of paper. Someone had typed up the conditions for spotting a jubilee and she smiled. They all crowded around the old priest as he got out a very tall crab pot and filled it with water and threw in crab boil seasonings.

He waited patiently for it to boil, "Now young Florence, how about you be the first to grab a crab with these tongs here and put it in the water."

She shook her head, "Father, I just don't think that's going to happen."

Riley stepped up to the bucket, picked up a crab and dropped it in the water. He turned around and Florence was right there peeking behind his back at the crab he just submerged in the water.

She covered her ears, "Riley, I can hear it screaming."

He grinned at her, "Come on, try it. I bet deep down inside you'd like to put one in the water just to see how it works. I know that mind of yours, Florence. You're a teacher and you're curious." He held out the tongs to her.

She took the tongs, picked up a crab and slowly dropped it in the water. She quickly stepped back peeking down into the pot to see the crab's pincers flail for a moment and she covered her ears again, "Y'all can't hear it screaming? I swear it's eyes kept looking at me."

Riley' s mouth curved as he looked at her. She noticed his gaze on her and a smile formed on her face. They both stepped to the back of the group to give everyone a chance to put a crab in the pot. Florence sauntered over to the other side of the room to explore the framed photos of families on the wall.

Riley stood beside her, "These are all of the families that came to stay here over the years. Father had a lot of duties back then with his church being in Mobile. He wasn't living over here full time like he is now. So, he had a few trusted families he would allow to stay here. They were hard working families who did a lot for the church and were close to Father Murphy. They made sure the house was looked after and kept clean. Some of the men would come over to make sure that boards were replaced on the wharf and would scrape the barnacles off the steps out there leading down into the bay, so no one slipped."

Florence looked closer at the photos, "There's one of you and Hunt on a sailboat."

Hunt heard his name. He and Karen walked over to look at the picture, "Yes, Riley and I took that Sunfish out to sail."

Riley interrupted him, "It was a pitiful little boat, but we managed to have a lot of fun in it, didn't we?" He glanced at Hunt and they both grinned.

Father Jimmy came over to stare at the picture. He laughed, "Lads, remember the time I had to come pick you up in my fishing boat?" He looked at Hunt's parents and the sisters, "Their sailboat had tipped over. I happened to be working on my little boat and spied it going over.

These lads couldn't get it back upright, so I cranked my motor and off I went to the rescue." He shook his head as he chuckled.

Ollie put his hand on Father's shoulder, "Those were some good times. Remember the time my son closed his eyes while walking on the wharf just to see how far his feet could touch until he got to the edge?" Hunt's father shook his head.

Hunt turned red, "Dad, I was 8 years old. Didn't I open my eyes at the last second which saved me from going into the water?"

"That and me yelling at you to stop. You almost gave your mother here a heart attack."

Riley spoke up, "Hunt, remember the time we borrowed Father Murphy's little fishing boat and were coming back in? We thought we'd see how close we could bring her into the wharf without hitting it. Too bad the boat never slowed." Karen asked, "What happened?"

"At the last minute Hunt turned the boat, but not before it hit the pier. Father here was not happy with us. Luckily, it didn't damage the wharf."

Hunt picked up the story, "Our knuckles were raw from having to scrape barnacles off steps that summer and filling in the bulkhead that was washing out. Father was a big believer in penance. Right, Father Murphy?" The good old priest just smiled.

Karen eyed the pictures and saw one with three German shepherds standing next to Father Jimmy. "Father, are these your dogs?"

Father walked up and touched the picture, "Ah, lass, these were my dogs I had years ago. Fritz, Rena and Happy. They were good protectors."

Annie spoke up, "Yes, Father Jimmy, I remember that Happy was sweet because she was the mother of those two." She pointed to Fritz, "Now he was something else, that one. I went to put a bag of groceries down inside the rectory door and he nipped my knee. He sure was your protector, Father. From what I remember, Rena could be sweet when Fritz wasn't around."

"Yes, lass." He looked out the screen door towards the bay, "All three are buried in that yard out there so they can look at the bay as much as they want and remember the times, they swam there with me in that water." He laughed, "I had forgotten, but I used to bring soap out there with me and bathe them. They didn't like standing still too long for that, so I used to get you all to help me. Do you remember that Ollie?"

Ollie grinned, "Yes, I do. I almost got nipped by Fritz there. He wasn't one to want to take a bath. Now, Happy was the sweetest. She was good about standing there as long as it took."

Hunt joined in, "Riley, we got Rena one time. She was fine until Fritz came around and then they were thick as thieves in trying to cause trouble."

Father smiled and suggested they get on with cooking breakfast. Everyone helped. Eggs were scrambled, sausage was fried in the pan and crabmeat was picked out for crab omelets. The leftover crab bodies were saved for gumbo. Florence eyed the orange shells that covered the crabs. She was amazed that the colors of the shells changed when dropped into boiling water.

The cafeteria style table on the screen covered porch was covered with newspapers for easy clean up. The group sat with full plates and ate their fill while enjoying each other's company. Stories about life at the bay house were plentiful. The group laughed and would take a moment or two to gaze out at the bay. Father asked who wanted an Irish coffee.

Karen looked up and asked the old priest if she could help with that. He raised his bushy eyebrows as if to question her. She explained to Father Jimmy, "I work in a coffee shop and love to make Irish coffee. However, we can't put alcohol in ours." Her eyes twinkled.

"Well, come on then, lass. We'll compare recipes and I think we're safe to add a little of some good Irish juice if the spirits move us." He grinned, "After you try my version, the spirits may move you after all." Laughter rang out as she followed him into the kitchen.

Everyone helped in the cleanup of the table and the group walked with their coffees in hand out to the end of the wharf to watch the dawn arise. Riley leaned on the railing next to Florence. As the sun slowly rose above the trees, he covered her hand with his. She scooted a little closer to him, so their shoulders were touching. He looked out over the water and smiled.

Father Jimmy and Hunt happened to notice the movements of Riley and Florence and glanced at each other with a knowing look and a smile.

Karen happened to glance in the water and saw a green head emerge from the bottom of the bay, "Father Jimmy, is that what I think it is?"

"Oh, my child, that's just Fred." Everyone stared at the water, "He's been here for a long time. I think he knows exactly when I'm out here and comes for a visit, isn't that right lad?"

Karen glanced at the alligator, "Father, you don't get in the water with him, do you?"

"Now, lass, I may be old, but I haven't lost my faculties enough to do something like that, would I Fred? Make no bones about it, he'd just as soon eat my hand than to allow me to be near him in that water. No, lass I wouldn't do that. I like being on land with all my digits intact."

Karen sighed with relief, "That's good to know, Father."

"There was a time, lass, when I would be in that water many a day, but with the alligator population booming, I don't go in there anymore. Some of the neighbors have swimming pools so they can live near the water, but still have a safe place for their family to swim."

Riley let go of Florence's hand, "Are you ladies about ready to go? I hate to end a good morning, but I have to open the park soon."

"Duty calls young Riley, doesn't it?" Father Jimmy patted his cheek and told him not to be a stranger, "You lasses are welcome anytime. It was very nice to meet you." He looked at Ollie and Annie, "It's nice to have these young folks around, isn't it? Although it reminds me of all the years between us."

Annie hugged Father, "Now, Father Jimmy, you're young at heart. I haven't forgotten you holding that net earlier though. I'm going to do my best not to fuss at you, but you have to be careful so we can come to many more jubilees."

He hugged her back, "Annie girl, don't go troubling yourself about me. I'm as strong as an ox. Just ask your son, there. Right lad?"

Hunt smiled, "Now, old man, don't go involving me in all this. I don't need my dear mother mad at me." They all walked down the wharf. The girls hugged the priest and said goodbye to the Huntingtons. Riley opened the girls' doors for them.

Florence looked back at Father Jimmy, "We want to thank you again for our time here. We were never able to experience anything like this as children. It was a real eye opener." He nodded his head and winked at her.

Father Jimmy handed Riley a bag, "It's some crabs to take to your mother and Aunt Alice. You've got your cooler loaded, right lad? Just be careful with the lifting when you get back home. Wouldn't want you pulling any muscles. You've got that park to take care of. Here, take this." Father handed him a St. Christopher medal, "Safe travels home lad."

"Thanks, Father Murphy. I think the girls had a great first jubilee."

Hunt walked up to Riley, "Don't forget to back out slowly so you don't hit those pine trees lining the driveway." He glanced at the good old Irish priest.

"George Huntington don't be going on about my trees. I did

cut one down, if you remember."

He eyed Father Murphy, "Yes, Father, that was five years ago." The old priest's mouth curved as he looked at Hunt and Riley. Riley grinned as he got in his car and backed up perfectly. He waited for the cars on the road to pass. He and the girls waved to the group assembled in the driveway and then Riley pulled out onto the road. The Huntington family collected all their belongings and loaded coolers filled with fish into their car. Father handed them over two milk cartons filled with shrimp to freeze when they got home. They said their goodbyes and thanked Father Murphy. As the old Irish priest watched his dear friends depart his home, he retraced his steps back to the yard. He stood at the end of the wharf and looked up to heaven. He thanked God for all he had and would rejoice when his time came to leave his life here on earth.

He glanced back at his house. He had offers to sell his house and property. He knew it was worth a couple of million dollars, but he wouldn't part with it, not as long as there was still breath in his body. Father James Murphy eyed his home and thought about his plan of whom would inherit all of this when he died. He had no relatives left, but he had a pretty good idea what he was going to do. He just needed to get it on paper and have a lawyer make it all legal. He walked out to the crab wharf to talk it over with Fred.

Chapter 10

Florence was just thinking about how she loved this time of year as she let herself into her apartment. She and Karen had a great weekend staying at the TreeHouse and being a part of a jubilee. She also thought about her time with Riley at the bay. She felt something had sparked there. She'd have to see how things went. After all, he was still her boss.

Maybe it was the schoolteacher in her, but the fall always felt like starting over and looking at things in a fresh, new way. The fall leaves would be changing. Kids would be coming to school and chatting with friends and teachers they hadn't seen over the summer.

As Florence set her purse and bag on the bench by the door, she flung off her shoes and dropped onto the couch, making sure her phone was in reach in case someone called. Wow, she hadn't been this tired in a long time.

She thought about work. The park had shifted into fall and schools were already booking field trips. From what Toni had told her, there were special fall programs geared to the children interested in the science labs and in the farming area of the park. Florence had gotten used to being in the farming area since her first time seeing it with Riley. She had to make several trips there with her groups and realized she couldn't avoid it forever. Her sister Karen was right.

Keith's memory would always be a part of her life, but she had to move on. As she leaned her head back on the couch, she heard her phone ring. She sighed and picked up her phone and had to blink twice at the name of the caller on the other end--Riley Simmons.

"Hello Riley," said Florence as she answered the phone, "what can I do for you?"

As he held the phone and heard her question, a million thoughts came into Riley's head, some that required being very close to Florence Smith. He really enjoyed being at the bay with her.

"Riley?" he heard Florence ask.

"Hey," Riley said. "I just wanted to call to see if you and your sister would be interested in joining Hunt and myself Saturday night. It would be our treat. We're taking Aunt Alice out for dinner and dancing. I thought you might like to meet her seeing as you have a few things in common."

"And those few things in common would be?" Florence asked Riley with a smile on her face.

"Well," Riley said, "You both like to dance and you both have worked at the park."

You said a few things we have in common. You named two. What's the third?" Florence asked.

He thought to himself, "You both have a soft spot for me." But then thought better of it and replied, "You're both very tough women and know how to survive whatever life throws at you."

"Is that a compliment, Mr. Simmons?"

"Why yes, Miss Smith, I believe it is."

Before Florence could say anything, Riley replied, "Just don't get too used to it. Wouldn't want you to get a big ego or anything."

Florence couldn't help but smile on the other end of the phone. He was a real charmer and she needed to be very careful.

Riley asked, "Is that a yes?"

"I need to check with my sister, but I think we'd both be available. We could meet you there."

Riley grinned and said, "Great. Looking forward to Saturday night."

Before he could hang up, Florence asked, "Oh, by the way Riley, where should we meet you?"

Riley replied, "Swansons. See you later."

Florence hung up and dialed her sister. She picked up on the first ring.

"Hey sis," Karen said, "what's up?"

"We have dinner and dancing invitations for Saturday night and we need to get us some new dresses. You free for a shopping trip tomorrow evening?" Karen asked, "Depends, where's dinner?"

Florence told her the name of the restaurant and Karen replied, "Definitely, see you tomorrow night."

Saturday night came all too soon. As Karen and Florence drove past the bluff in Fairhope, they both glanced at the bay and sighed. There were sailboats on the water, people walking on the pier, and families riding bicycles on the sidewalks.

Karen was the first to speak, "What a beautiful sunset. Just gorgeous."

"I know," sighed Florence, "It's like a different world over here, peaceful and one of the greatest places to watch the sunset."

Karen looked down at her black dress, perfect for any occasion, "By the way, thanks for the dress. I owe you."

"Well, it's not every day an invitation to Swanson's comes along. Don't give it another thought." replied Florence, as she glanced at her sister.

Florence and Karen studied their surroundings as they drove past sections of rental houses for tourists, ice cream shops, and art galleries eventually winding their way past stately homes and mansions that have belonged to local families for generations.

Finally reaching their destination, Florence turned down a long winding driveway, lined with ancient oak trees that were old enough to tell stories about the generations of the families.

There, beyond the clearing was a majestic two-story waterfront home with stately columns and a fountain designed by a famous local artist. As families moved away, the home was sold and opened as an elegant restaurant by the Swanson family. As Florence pulled around the circular driveway and stopped the car, valets opened the doors for both ladies. Florence and Karen walked through the front door, and the opulence took their breath away.

Gold and white seemed to be the color scheme, with the focal point being a large, customized chandelier in the front foyer along with many antique furnishings.

Karen remarked, "Just beautiful." Florence agreed.

The sisters checked in with the Maître D' at the front desk

and were soon being led to their table. Florence eyed the elegant white tablecloths and the colorful flower arrangements on each table. The band in white tie and tails reminded her of the big band era. Perfectly enough, the band was playing big band era music.

Seated at their table, Riley had been checking his watch. His Aunt Alice asked, "Riley, that is the third time you have checked your watch. Why so impatient?" At that moment Riley looked around the room and stood up from the table. Hunt stood up as well.

Aunt Alice looked up and said with a twinkle in her eye, "Oh, now I see why." Riley watched Florence walk to the table and his brain stopped functioning.

He was at a loss for words. She was stunning in a blue V-neck cocktail dress with a silver brooch pinned over her waist. Her hair was piled on top of her head in a devil-may-care way that was considered by Riley as being exceptionally sexy on her.

As the ladies reached their table, Riley found his voice, "Well, hello there. You ladies look absolutely beautiful." Riley looked around the table, "We're glad you could join us." Karen and Florence both waved at Hunt. Hunt inclined his head and said, "Ladies,"

The waiter seated the ladies next to each other. Florence glanced at the striking older lady wearing a long off-white antique lace dress seated at the end of the table. She had fluffy white hair and the most beautiful, porcelain skin she had ever seen.

Riley took his seat next to Hunt, cleared his throat, and made the introductions.

"Aunt Alice, I would like you to meet Florence Smith. She works at the park as an educator." Turning to the brunette, he said, "This is her sister, Karen."

Aunt Alice turned to both sisters and asked, "How do you do? It's very nice to meet you both."

Florence smiled, "It's nice to meet you as well. I've heard a lot about you from Riley." She noticed an older lady sitting at the table next to Aunt Alice. She had curly red hair with a curvy figure that could rival any lady in the room.

Aunt Alice turned to her companion, "I would like you to meet my best friend, Elmira." Elmira spoke up, "Nice to meet you gals. Are you from the area?"

Karen answered, "Yes, we grew up across the bay." Before anyone could say anything else, the waiter placed a decanter of water on the table and asked if any of the group would care for any drinks.

"Aunt Alice?" Riley asked, "What would you like?"

"Oh, Riley, you know what I like," as Aunt Alice looked at the waiter she said, "young man, I'll have a Sazerac." As the waiter took the rest of the drink orders, Florence saw Riley watching her.

She couldn't help but notice him as well, in a crisp navy business suit with a white buttoned-down shirt. He sported a navy and pink tie along with a crisp matching pocket square. He looked sexy as hell. She noticed a design on his tie and his pocket square--pink flamingos. She looked up and caught him staring at her. She nodded toward the tie and smiled. He grinned. Aunt Alice caught the looks between Florence and Riley and tapped Elmira's foot under the table. She had caught the looks as well. She turned to Alice with a twinkle in her eye.

Karen was the first to break the silence, "Well, Hunt, how have you been?"

Hunt replied, “Can’t complain. There’s never a shortage of coughs, colds, or sprained ankles, so I stay busy. How about yourself?”

Karen answered, “I hope to finish school soon and start sending out resumes for jobs in my field.”

Aunt Alice looked at Karen and asked, “What are you studying, dear?”

“I’m almost finished with my master’s degree in Speech Language Pathology at South.

Until I can get my dream job, I’ve been working at a coffee shop in Daphne.”

Elmira asked,” You mean Good to the Last Drop?” Karen nodded. Elmira went on and on all about her favorite coffees from there. She turned to Alice, “Alice, we’ve been there.

Remember? We got those fabulous, iced coffees from there a couple of weeks ago. Well, honey, next time we come by we’ll be sure to say hello now that we know who you are!”

“Yes ma’am,” said Karen,” I hope to see you there on your next trip.” A moment later the drinks arrived at the table and the waiter took everyone’s order.

The Maitre’D leaned down and whispered in Hunt’s ear, “Great idea. Thank you, Thomas. Ladies, I’ve just been told there’s a spectacle to behold on the west side of the porch. Would you all like to see?” The ladies got up from their chairs as the men, with Thomas’s guidance down a private hallway, escorted them to the wrap around porch. The reflection of the moon on the bay glowed as thought it had a life of its own. The lights of the city of Mobile reflected on the bay so those admiring the view couldn’t tell where the city stopped, and the bay began. On the trees and bushes on either side of the porch, thousands of fireflies appeared. It was as if mother nature was putting on a show just for them. Riley was surprised when his hand, seemingly of its own volition, reached over to Florence's. He was even more surprised when her fingers entwined with his. The group stood silently for what could have been hours or minutes. Florence and Riley felt as if everything and everyone had fallen away as though they were the only ones there.

The Maitre'D arrived and broke the spell, "Your food will be ready momentarily, if you all would like to follow me back to the table." Riley and Florence dropped their hands to their sides. Aunt Alice and Elmira, eyes sharp as ever, noticed the movement. Aunt Alice looked at Elmira and smiled. Elmira chuckled softly.

Everyone settled themselves at the table and picked up their drinks.

As everyone sipped on their drinks, the band began to play Moon River. A young man stepped up to the microphone and began to sing, "Moon river, wider than a mile, I'm crossing you in style someday..."

Riley looked at his Aunt Alice. She glanced at him.

He stood up, walked to Aunt Alice's chair, and held his hand out, "Aunt Alice, may I have this dance?"

Aunt Alice reached up and patted his cheek and said, "Yes you may."

As the young man continued to sing, Riley led Aunt Alice onto the dance floor. Elmira's eyes shone with tears as she looked at Karen, Florence and Hunt, "This was Alice and Frank's song that they danced to at their wedding. It was their first dance." Hunt nodded and smiled.

Riley held Aunt Alice's hand and turned her in a small

circle, and they began to waltz.

"Two drifters, off to see the world, there's such a lot of world to see…."

As Riley danced with his aunt, the room filled with people watching the couple glide around the dance floor. "We're after the same rainbow's end, waitin' 'round the bend. My huckleberry friend, moon river and me…."

Florence watched Riley and his aunt. She felt a tear fall down her cheek, "Oh damn," she thought. She was falling in love with Riley Simmons.

As the dance ended, there wasn't a dry eye in the room. Riley looked at his Aunt, who had tears in her eyes. He touched her cheek and said, "I loved him too, Aunt Alice." This prompted more tears from his aunt. He smiled at her and gave her his handkerchief square from his pocket.

She hugged him tight and then looked at him, "You're a good boy, Riley Simmons. I only hope you meet someone to love as much as I loved your uncle." Riley saw her nod her head towards Florence at the table and she said, "From the way you keep looking at young Florence, I'd say you're on your way."

Riley was speechless. He thought, "Is it really that obvious?"

As Riley led his aunt back to their table, the waiters arrived with their meals. After making sure his aunt was seated, he happened to look up and noticed Florence wipe her eyes with a tissue. She glanced at him and gave him a slow smile. He looked at her and winked. Aunt Alice and Elmira saw the looks pass between Riley and Florence. The two women smiled and clinked their glasses together.

As everyone was finishing their meals, Karen and Florence

looked up as the announcer tapped on the bandstand. The band stopped playing. "Excuse me ladies and gentlemen, but I would like to make an announcement. As we like to do here at Swanson's, we want to acknowledge a celebration. Would Mr. and Mrs. Gershwin please stand?" Florence watched a very fit couple who looked to be in their early 50's smile and rise from their chairs. They were dressed in evening attire. She had on a wrist corsage and he had a single red rose pinned to his suit lapel.

The announcer continued, "The Gershwins are celebrating their 30th wedding anniversary." The announcer paused while everyone clapped. He looked at the couple, "Your children, friends and relatives at your table want to let you know of their love for you and want to thank you for being the wonderful parents, friends and relations that you are." This was met with more clapping from the people seated in the restaurant. The Gershwins looked around the table, smiled, nodded to the announcer and were about to sit down, "Before you get comfortable, there is one request from your children. They would like you to dance, but not just any dance.

Mr. and Mrs. Gershwin, please step to the center of the dance floor." The Gershwins looked at their children as the teenagers just grinned. The room went wild with laughter and more clapping.

As the couple entered the dance floor, the announcer spoke to them and said, "Remember, your children did this. You can always take away their car keys later!" Laughter filled the room. "The children have picked out a disco song for their parents. I understand the Gershwins are ballroom dance studio owners, so this should be fun to watch! Let's celebrate the Gershwins, whose love is real." He gestured to the band, "Hit it!"

The music started and the couple on the dance floor started laughing.

The sounds of Cheryl Lynn's disco song, "To Be Real" flooded over the room.

The Gershwins began to move. The couple held hands and bumped hips together as the band played and their table sang the lyrics along with the music "What you think now, I think I love you baby, what you feel now, I think I need you baby...to be real!"

The couple finished their dance, moved to the side, and waved everyone on to the dance floor. The Gershwin's' teenagers and their friends skipped to the dance floor and began to jump up and pump their fists into the air to the music.

Riley looked at Hunt and they both looked at Florence and Karen, "Are you ladies up for some disco?"

Karen and Florence looked at each other, then at Aunt Alice.

Aunt Alice said, "You kids go enjoy yourselves, disco is for the young." Then she smiled.

Hunt helped Karen from her chair, and they moved onto the dance floor to join the teenagers and their family.

Riley held out his hand, "Well, Florence, what do you say?"

Florence looked at Riley, held out her hand and said, "Sure, but let's see if you can keep up with me."

Riley took her hand and smiled, "Just watch me."

Alice and Elmira watched Riley and Florence walk to the dance floor. "So," Elmira said, sipping her cocktail, "what do you think their chances are?"

Alice replied, "I think they're goners." Elmira winked at Alice, "Me too." They both laughed.

As the music continued, Riley, Florence, Hunt and Karen found themselves joining the teenagers on the dance floor. The dancers began to pair off to finish the dancing. Florence found herself in Riley's arms as they began to dance. He held her in his arms, and both moved like they had been together for years.

Riley spun Florence around as she landed back in his arms. As the music ended, she settled her arms on top of his and held on. Florence turned her head to look at Riley. She could feel his heart beating against her back. It's almost as if time stopped and neither of them moved until they heard the sound of clapping. They looked around and realized people were clapping for them. They separated, smiled, and bowed.

Hunt reached Riley and put his hand on his shoulder, "Man that was really something."

Karen came up to Florence and hugged her. She looked at Hunt and said, "Told you she was a phenomenal dancer!"

As the couples made it back to the table, Aunt Alice looked at them and exclaimed, "Bravo!"

Riley reached for his water glass; he was interrupted by the couple who had the anniversary, "Hi, we just wanted to stop by your table and let you know that you are extremely talented."

Riley looked at Florence and Aunt Alice and said to the Gershwins, "It helps to have partners that make me look good!" Everyone laughed.

Mr. Gershwin looked at Aunt Alice and said, "My wife and I really enjoyed watching you two waltz. I think you're a professional dancer."

Aunt Alice remarked, "I have a background in dance. Once upon a time, I was a dancer at the Sunset Jubilee Theme Park." She nodded towards Riley, "My nephew here now runs the park."

"Oh!" Mrs. Gershwin exclaimed, "We used to take the kids

there all the time when they were little."

Mr. Gershwin said, "That was a long time ago, wasn't it?"

Riley looked at his Aunt Alice. She glanced at him and nodded her head. Riley turned in his seat to look at the Gershwins, "I'll tell you what. Since this is your 30th Anniversary, how about a weekend at the park for old times' sake? Just the two of you? My treat?" The couple looked at each other.

Riley sweetened the deal, "It would mean two weekend passes to the park plus two nights' accommodations."

The couple both laughed and said, "Ok!"

Riley reached into his wallet, pulled out his business card, and gave it to the Gershwins with instructions to call his number to set up the visit. Riley said to Mr. Gershwin,"If you would give me your name, I'll put it in my phone as a reminder for when you call."

The couple looked at each other and Mr. Gershwin sighed, "My first name is Ira." Everyone at the table stared at him, "Yes, I know, but my mom is a cellist with the symphony and was a huge fan. I also have a brother named George." Everyone laughed.

Ira glanced at Riley, "Thank you again and we'll certainly be in touch with you." He looked at his wife, took her hand and asked, "Ready to go?"

His wife hesitated, looked at Riley and said, "One more question before we go. What kind of overnight accommodations do you have at the park?"

Riley looked around the table, smiled at everyone and then turned back to the couple, "How do you feel about treehouses?"

Chapter 11

The weekend that everyone had been waiting for had finally arrived. The Fall Extravaganza Weekend was in full swing as Riley drove the golf cart through the park on a beautiful Saturday morning. Banners emblazoned with pumpkins and fall leaves had been carefully placed all through the park. He waved as he recognized old friends and acquaintances. As he drove by each area, he saw children's faces smeared with cotton candy and ice cream.

He watched parents pushing strollers, teenagers with air pods stride by, and senior citizens sitting on benches in the shade passing the time. It was turning out to be a good day.

The park crew had done a great job with the set-ups. Kiosks had been placed all through the park with crew members selling park merchandise, baked goods, and walking sticks. He had given his employees who only worked during the week the option of overtime by working extra hours on the weekend.

Riley found himself driving up to the Founding Farmers area. Every time he came through this area now, he would think of Florence. He got out of the golf cart to walk through the field towards the greenhouse area. Florence never did share her story with him the first time she toured the farming venue. He thought about dancing with her at Swanson's. He was going to try his best to dance with her again. As Riley looked around, pumpkins were spilling out of crates, apple hand pies were selling like hotcakes at the bakery booth, and guests were milling about the barn. Baskets of yellow and orange mums were quickly sold to guests excited to place these on their front porches at home. Once he spotted the mums, he found the woman he was looking for.

He waited until she noticed him, “Riley!” He stepped closer and hugged the small woman with a head full of brown curls and bright blue eyes, “Hi mom,” Riley said, “How are things?”

Mary Simmons hugged her son back and said, “Business is blooming!” Riley groaned and rolled his eyes, “Mom, that was the worst pun ever!!”

“I know,” Mary elbowed Riley, “but you have to admit it was just a little funny! Come on, that’s mom humor. There is an understood rule that whenever your mom makes a joke, you have to laugh at it.”

Riley chuckled and asked, “Who made that rule?”

Mary tugged at her hair, “Moms did so they could get back at their children who gave them all this gray hair!” Riley laughed. There was no one quite like his mother. She looked forward to this weekend every year.

Riley looked around, “Looks like the flowers and plants are big sellers today.”

“Yes, sir,” said Mary, “It’s been a good morning. Let’s hope it stays that way.” As Mary moved more mums up to the front of the sales area, she said, “Oh, I’m sorry I couldn’t make the dinner at Swanson’s. I understand from Alice that your dancing was a hit! It sounds like she had a great time. I’m so glad you two are close. It makes me happy.” Riley bided his time. He didn’t have to wait long, “So,” Mary said very casually, “tell me about this new lady in your life, Florence, is it? I heard she's very beautiful and a wonderful dancer. I also heard she makes my son smile and that during dinner he couldn't take his eyes off her." His mom gave him a look.

"And there it is," said Riley.

"There what is? "asked Mary, the picture of innocence.

"Aunt Alice needs a new hobby besides gossiping about her nephew to his mother," said Riley, "Are we really going down this road?" His mom just looked at him.

"Mom, she works for me." Riley sighed as he didn't want to explain his feelings about Florence to his mom. He wasn't even sure what those feelings were. He liked holding her in his arms when they danced. He liked it when she smiled, which was rare when he was around. When he was on the receiving end of one of those smiles, it made his week.

His mom nudged his arm and said, "That sure is a lot of thinkin' you're doing."

"I really don't know what you expect me to say. Yes, she's beautiful, smart, and talented. However, my focus right now needs to be on keeping this park a success. It's not easy living up to what my uncle and father did."

"Oh, Riley," his mom remarked," I want so much more for you. I know your father and uncle left big shoes to fill. I'm so sorry they left too soon." She put her hand on his arm, "Riley, they had so much more than the park, even though it was a big part of their life. They both found someone to love." As she looked up at her son, she said, "I want you to have that, too. I want someone to know what a wonderful man you are and how lucky that person would be to have you in their life. Plus, I wouldn't mind having some grandchildren sometime in the near future. You know I'm not getting any younger."

Riley looked at his mom and pulled her in for a hug, “I don’t know what I’d do without you.” He kissed the top of her head.

Mary said, “Well I do have some thoughts on that subject if you care to hear them.” She glanced up and smiled at her son with a twinkle in her eye and said, “I still wouldn’t mind meeting Florence. Why don’t you take a little time and think about it?”

Riley was about to reply when he observed Florence walking into the Founding Farmers area. He eyed his mother and replied, “Well, it looks like I won’t need any time to think about this. Can you get someone to cover for you so I can make introductions?”

“You bet, hang on a minute,” she uttered as she disappeared into the flower tent, “Ok, all set!”

Florence didn’t have any groups until the afternoon and since she was meeting someone, she decided the best place to wait would be at the rodeo entrance. She was leaning on the wooden fence watching the calf roping event. Florence had been told the rodeo was held once a year to raise money for local charities. Colorfully dressed rodeo clowns were starting to enter the circle. They were waving their hats, squirting water out of flowers, and some were peddling unicycles. Florence really liked clowns. She thought they were hilarious. Watching the clowns made her think of Riley, and she smiled.

He was always a surprise. He gave kids a chance when no one else would and he worked hard to make sure guests left the park wanting to come back again. She also couldn’t forget how he made her feel when he danced with her. She felt alive. She also couldn’t shake the fact that maybe that was a betrayal to Keith. She hadn’t been with anyone since Keith. Every year the heartache seemed to lessen a little bit more. Florence had been thinking a lot about him the last few days. Maybe it had something to do with who she was meeting today. She was so lost in thought she was startled when she felt a hand touch her arm. As she faced the man that had become a true friend since Keith's death, she leaned into his arms and gave him a big hug.

He held on and said, "Hi there kiddo. It's been a long time." "Curtis! I'm so glad you called me! It has been a long time."

Curtis Dalton, Keith's brother, released Florence and said, "Well, now. You're a sight for sore eyes. When did you get so pretty?" Florence swatted his arm and asked, "What, was I that ugly before?"

Curtis laughed and answered her, "Oh, Florence, I've missed you." Florence smiled, "I've missed you too, Curtis."

Riley was close enough to catch the conversation between Florence and a man she seemed very close with. Funny, she never mentioned a man named Curtis. He looked to be a little older than Florence. Of course, she didn't have to divulge all of her past to him as Riley was her boss and nothing but her boss. In all his time spent with Florence he had been enthralled, with her sense of humor, her kindness to children, and her energy.

Though Riley had stressed to his mom that Florence was his employee, even his mom had guessed there was something more. Riley had thought maybe in time there could be but watching Florence with this Curtis left room for doubt.

Florence was deep in conversation with Curtis, when she happened to notice a couple standing behind them, "Hello Riley!" Florence exclaimed. Curtis turned at the same time Florence spoke to a man standing with an older lady who resembled him.

"Florence," Riley nodded his head, "I happened to see you across the field and thought I would introduce you to my mother. Mom, this is Florence Smith. Florence, this is my mom, Mary

Simmons."

Florence peered at the woman with brown curls and blue eyes. She'd seen those blue eyes before, in her boss's face, who was staring at the man she was with at the moment.

Florence shook Mary's hand, "It's so nice to meet you. Since I've been here, I've been able to learn the history of the park and your family's role in building it from the ground up."

"Well, dear," Mary said as she held Florence's hand, "I'm glad I could meet you as well. Alice told me she really enjoyed meeting you at dinner. Alice said watching you dance that night brought back many fond memories of her time at the park."

Curtis, who had been quiet up until this point, broke his silence, "Oh, my family always thought Florence here could have been on Broadway as a dancer if she hadn't gone into teaching."

Florence looked at Curtis and said, "Oh, I'm so sorry. Curtis Dalton, this is Mary and Riley Simmons. Riley is my boss. His family built this park. Curtis is..." Florence was at a loss for words.

Curtis finished for her, "I'm an old family friend. I haven't seen Florence in a while and thought we'd catch up for old times' sake."

As Riley continued to remain silent, his mother gave him a look and spoke up, "Well, Curtis, you sure did pick a great weekend to visit. This is our yearly Fall Extravaganza and there's a lot to see in the park. We're packed on this weekend every year."

"Yes, ma'am, I could see that when I came in the park." Curtis noticed Florence and Riley make eye contact. Curtis looked at Riley and said, "I like what you've done here with the farming area. My brother, sister and I grew up on a big farm in the county and this brings back memories. Especially the rodeo, that's a nice touch."

Riley pulled his gaze away from Florence, looked at Curtis and said, "Thank you. We like it and the guests who come through here seem to like it." Riley watched Florence.

Florence glanced away and said, "I did promise Curtis a tour of the park before my afternoon group sessions." Florence looked at Riley's mom, "Mrs. Simmons, it was very nice to meet you."

"Oh dear, please call me Mary. I hope we'll run into each other again."

As Florence nodded, Curtis held out his hand. "Riley, is it?" Riley nodded and looked at Curtis for a long second before shaking his hand. Curtis nodded his head at Riley's mom and said,

"Ma'am, it was nice meeting you." Mary glanced at Curtis, smiled and said, "Likewise. You kids have a good tour."

Florence gazed at Riley then walked off with Curtis.

Mary focused on her son and asked, "Riley Justin Simmons, did you lose your manners somewhere between the flower tent and the rodeo fence? You hardly said two words to Florence and her friend." Riley was quiet as he saw Florence and her "friend" leave the farm area.

Mary asked, "Is there something I don't know that you'd like to tell me?"

Riley looked at his mom and answered, "Well, mom, first there has to be something to tell and from where I'm standing, there doesn't seem much to talk about."

"Riley, I saw the looks you two were giving each other.

There's a story there somewhere.

You didn't seem happy to see her with her friend." Riley remained quiet so Mary decided to poke the bear, "He's a handsome fellow and she's a very pretty girl. I can see why they're friends."

Riley regarded his mom and decided it was time to change the subject. He eyeballed the flower tent and said to his mom, "Looks like business is blooming! Why don't we get you back to work?"

Riley's mom could hear the sarcasm from her son, but she gave him a sly smile, "Oh, they'll be another time to finish our talk, Riley. You should know by now; moms don't give up that easily." She patted his cheek and let him lead her back to the flowers.

Florence was quiet as she escorted Curtis through the other areas of the park.

"Florence, let's sit for a minute." He looked at the waterfall behind them and sat on the bench next to Florence.

Florence gazed at Curtis and said, "Curtis, listen, I..." she stammered and couldn't finish her thought.

Curtis squeezed her hand and asked, "He's the one, isn't he Florence?" She swallowed, "The one?"

"Yes," Curtis answered, "The one you couldn't take your eyes off and the one who couldn't take his eyes off of you either. The one you've finally found who can chase away the sadness and pain of you losing my brother." Tears ran down Florence's face. Curtis hugged her to him and said, "Oh, honey, we all miss him, every day. Sometimes I catch mom forgetting and setting an extra place on the table for dinner. I see it in dad when he looks over at the fields with a sad expression on his face. I sometimes catch myself carrying on a conversation with Keith when I'm in the stables and believe me, you should see the strange looks I used to get from the groomer. Now, I try to make sure there's a horse around, so he thinks I'm talking to the horse."

Florence laughed through her tears and hugged him back, "Oh Curtis, I've really missed you. I'm so sorry I stopped visiting the farm." Florence said as a shadow came over her face and she lowered her head,

"Listen honey," Curtis said, "we all understand." Florence didn't respond. "Florence, look at me." Florence turned towards Curtis. "Keith will always be your first great love and you will always be a part of our family. But time moves on, and you've always given a big part of your heart to the children you teach.

It's time to give the other part to someone you can share your life with and who will love you back." As Curtis pointed behind him, he added, "Hopefully, the guy I met back there will learn that I'm not in the running to replace my brother, so he won't act like such a jackass if I run into him again on my next visit."

Florence wiped her eyes and laughed, "He's usually not such a jackass. He's actually a pretty good guy, most of the time." Florence smiled at Curtis.

"Is he now?" Curtis smiled, "He better be, because you deserve all the happiness there is in the world after the childhood you had and after losing Keith."

Florence hugged Curtis and said, "Thank you Curtis. You always know just what to say and what you say always seems to make sense."

Curtis hugged Florence back and said, "Well, most of the time it does, except when I get caught talking to the horses."

They looked at each other and laughed.

Jerry Smith had found a place to stay through an old cellmate. It was an old, rundown trailer not far from the interstate. It belonged to the cellmate's grandmother, who recently died, and it was abandoned. He told Jerry he was welcome to live there because he had taken a job with a trucking company up north and decided he wasn't coming back to live in the area.

Jerry looked around the yard. He saw rusted parts of bicycles and old cans that littered the driveway. He walked into the trailer and saw dishes piled in the sink, an old heater with rust on the bottom, and a living room with a pull-out couch that looked like it had seen better days. He looked around in disgust and thought about his own house that his sister-in-law still lived in. He knew she still lived there because he'd managed to pay for a cab from the money he had in his personal effects given back to him when he left the jail.

He wore an old Peterbilt hat someone had lost at the jail and glasses so he wouldn't be recognized. Jerry happened to spot his sister-in-law's car. It was the same piece of crap she had driven for years. He hadn't seen anyone else. He looked around the trailer. He didn't have much money left and sooner or later he was going to have to figure out another means of transportation. He knew a couple of buddies who stole cars for a living and could probably see if he could "borrow a car" especially once he got his money back that was still hidden in the ceiling in his house. Jerry walked over to the front door of the trailer and sat down on what passed as steps. He rubbed his beard and thought about his plan. It was about time to get reacquainted with the family.

Chapter 12

Sunday dawned bright and early. The second day of the Fall Extravaganza Weekend was in full swing. Riley zipped his golf cart through a private maintenance road in the park and thought about Florence. Once she walked off with her friend, he hadn't seen or spoken to her since yesterday. He needed to get a grip. So, what if she and her friend seemed to be happy with each other. So what? "So, what, plenty," he thought.

If he was honest with himself, he wanted to be the one on the receiving end of those hugs and Florence's laughter. He wanted her face to light up when she was around him instead of the other guy. Riley stopped the cart and turned the key. He laid his head on the steering wheel.

Maybe it was time to lay his cards on the table and have a talk with Florence. After his conversation with his mom yesterday, he realized he acted like an ass in front of Florence.

He lifted his head up. Maybe this guy was just a friend and nothing more. Maybe he still had a chance with her. It was time to find out, he thought to himself, as he turned the key and continued his ride down the road.

Florence had finished teaching her last group by noon, just in time to get something to eat. She tried to talk her mom and Ed into coming by the park today, but they were away for the weekend. Her sister would be meeting her that afternoon to watch the parade. Until then, she was going to enjoy herself. She spotted a booth selling corn dogs and made her way over.

Florence happily munched on her corndog as she took her time looking at all the decorations. The park crew really outdid themselves. It was just beautiful.

She had finished her corndog and was rounding the corner to the Welcome Station when she collided with a man who reached out his arms to steady her, "I'm sorry Miss, I was in too much of a hurry. Oh, Florence, it's you."

Florence saw that the man who collided with her was none other than her boss. She dropped her arms from holding his and said, "Hello Riley."

For a minute Riley said nothing. All he could do was stare at her and thought how beautiful she truly was and how glad he was to see her, "Um, listen Florence, about yesterday, I acted like a jerk and I wanted to apologize to you."

Florence gazed at Riley silently.

Riley sighed and asked, "You're going to make this really hard on me, aren't you?"

Florence replied, "Yep."

He spoke up again, "Just to clarify, you aren't going to make this easy for me?" Florence shook her head and said, "Nope."

Riley looked around and then he glanced back at Florence and took a deep breath. "Look," Riley said, "when I saw you with that guy…."

"His name is Curtis. He's a friend of mine, Riley."

"Okay, Florence. When I saw you with Curtis, I realized I didn't like what I saw."

"What do you mean you didn't like what you saw?"

Riley took another breath and went for it, "Well, you were laughing with him and hugging him."

Florence looked at her boss and said, "Riley, I've known him a long time. We're friends. Why would you have a hard time with that?"

Riley glanced away and finally turned his blue eyes to Florence, took a step forward and held her arms. He replied, "I have a hard time with it because I want to be the one you laugh with." He took a step closer to Florence. She held her breath, "I want to be the one who hugs you." Riley moved even closer, "Because I want to be the one who touches you." Florence looked into Riley's beautiful blue eyes, took a deep breath, and put her hands on his arms and leaned forward.

Just then the train whistle blew and startled them both.

Riley gazed at Florence, sighed, stepped back and muttered, "One of these days there won't be any interruptions." Riley looked down the main street and rubbed the back of his neck. "Listen," Riley said, "It's about an hour to parade time and I was headed over that way to check on things. Would you walk with me?"

Florence looked at Riley and said, "Well, I guess I can do that since you apologized so nicely." Then she smiled.

"Oh, Miss Smith, you really made me work for that one, didn't you?" Riley's mouth curved as they started their walk.

Chapter 13

Riley and Florence made it to the float pavilion when one of the managing float crew, who looked to Florence to be all of sixteen years old, met Riley at the door. "Mr. Simmons, we have a problem, sir."

"What's the problem Cecil?"

"We had everyone lined up in their spots, but the couple who are supposed to be the premiere dancers ---well, Cynthia is in the back bathroom throwing up and Carl sprained his ankle when he slipped off the ladder getting on the float."

Riley rubbed the back of his neck, took a deep breath, and asked, "Ok, Cecil, which float are they on and what's the dance number?"

Cecil looked at his clipboard and said, "It's the Country Jamboree float. The dance number involves a version of "If You're Going to Play in Texas" --you know, sir, the song with the fiddle. Everybody else is in place. The dancers are set to dance in front of the float." Cecil blew out a breath.

While Riley was trying to figure out what he was going to do, Florence had been texting her sister with her location. Riley observed Cecil after hearing the description for what was needed and asked, "Not complicated at all, huh?" Riley thought a minute, then rattled off the names of substitute dancers, "June, Teddy, Menka, John... any of them available?"

Cecil thought about that and shook his head, "No sir, they have prior commitments or are out of town." Riley shook his head and glanced at Florence. He watched her greet her sister,

Karen. Karen waved to Riley and he waved back.

"Flo, what's up? Why did you want me to meet you all the way over here?" inquired Karen. Florence explained the problem to her. She happened to glance at Riley who had his hands resting on his hips looking at her intently.

Karen caught the look, bumped Florence with her elbow and questioned, "Why is Riley staring at you like that?"

As Riley started walking their way, Florence said, "I think we're about to find out."

Riley said hello to Karen and then turned his attention to Florence, "Ok," he said, "here's the deal. I have two of my primary dancers down, all of my fill-in dancers are otherwise engaged, the parade starts in forty-five minutes...." Florence was shaking her head as Riley was talking. "Hear me out," Riley said as Florence continued to shake her head, "We have about half an hour to learn the routine. I already know we can dance together, so I think we can do this."

Florence asked, "You and me? You want me to dance with you in one of the biggest parades in this area and learn the routine in thirty minutes? Are you crazy?"

"Crazy like a fox, yes, if it means keeping this parade going." Riley took a deep breath and continued trying to convince her to do this today, "Florence, did you see how many guests are in this park today? People wait all year for this weekend. It's very important to this community and it's important all of our events go off without a hitch. Guests that are here for the weekend may come back again, and that's what helps keep us going for the year."

As Riley wound down his plea to Florence, Karen asked, "So, what's the dance?"

Riley repeated what his crew manager had told him earlier about the music, the float set up, and the dance routine,

"Oh, Flo! You got this. Remember when you took me along with your friends for country night at the Civic Center and we learned all those dances? You'd be great!" Karen got a look from her sister and said, "Sorry, I'll just stand over here and mind my own business."

"Look," Riley implored, "Cecil has the video of the dress rehearsal. We can watch it and still have time to practice and get into our costumes. With your dancing skills, I know we can pull this off. What do you say, Florence? I really could use your help here." Riley glanced at his watch, "Time's ticking."

Florence looked up at Riley and exclaimed, "Oh, hell, I'm really going do this, aren't I?

Let's go."

She was shaking her head as Riley stepped forward, picked her up and spun her around in a circle,.

"Riley, what the blazes?" Florence said as she slid down his body and her feet touched the ground.

Riley had the biggest grin on his face, "Florence Smith, you've just made my day. I can't thank you enough!"

Florence had to interrupt him, pointed to her watch, and said, "Riley, time's ticking!"

Riley smiled at her, "Yes ma'am. Let's do this!

As he led Florence away, she called to Karen, "See you on Sunshine Street."

"Have fun!" Karen called out to Flo. She started walking to find a place in the front to see her sister dance.

Everyone was in place. Florence stared at the big float behind her.

"Don't worry," Riley said standing next to her in a cowboy hat, a red bandana and the flashiest boots she'd ever seen, "you're a safe distance from that float and Cecil knows what he's doing."

Florence looked back at Riley, arched an eyebrow and said, "Oh, I'm not worried about the float. Just worried you might not be able to keep up." She glanced down at his boots and looked back at him, "Wouldn't want you to throw your back out, blow a knee, sprain an ankle." She checked him out and added, "You are getting up there in age."

Riley looked at Florence and his gaze travelled from her cowboy hat perched on top of her head, down to the red bandana that matched the one Riley was wearing. His eyes continued gazing at the longest legs he'd ever seen. As his eyes travelled back up to her face, he said, "Oh, don't you worry Florence. I'm in top physical condition."

Florence could feel her face blush from Riley's perusal of her body, "Really? Huh," Florence remarked, "I guess we'll see. By the way, nice boots." she smirked.

"Nice legs," he grinned.

As the parade began, Riley glanced at Florence and said, "Here we go!"

The parade proceeded down Sunshine Street. The crowd laughed and clapped along with the music. Float after float rolled down the street, with guests catching beads decorated with fall motifs, state football teams and the rare, but coveted sunshine emblem beads. If caught, the emblem beads entitled the guest to a complimentary weekend at the park for two.

The Country Jamboree float found its way to the top of Sunshine Street and stopped so the attention was focused on the dancers. As the music started, the singer on the top began to sing his song, "If you're going to play in Texas, you gotta have a fiddle in the band…."

All the dancers started weaving in and out with a square dance. As Riley and Florence took their steps to promenade by the VIP section, they danced by his mom, his aunt and Karen, all standing together, waving to them. Riley and Florence smiled at them all as Aunt Alice blew them a kiss.

Florence jumped into Riley's arms and he spun her around. As they danced together, they couldn't take their eyes off one another. Every touch heightened their awareness. Every look seemed like a caress. As the song ended, the dancers shifted back in a line holding hands and waving to the crowds. Riley held on tight to Florence's hand as they walked down Sunshine Street. As the floats moved back into the barn and the dancers dispersed, Riley and Florence continued to walk hand and hand through the side of the barn and up the stairs. When they reached the landing near the upstairs office, Riley turned to face Florence. She took off her cowboy hat. Riley reached up and tucked a tendril of hair off her face and behind her ear. His hand caressed her cheek and lingered there. She put her hand over his.

"Florence," breathed Riley. Florence put her other hand on Riley's chest and looked into those beautiful blue eyes. He took her hand, raised it up and kissed the palm of her hand.

At that moment, a surge of staff who were in the parade

streamed through the barn doors downstairs.

Riley touched Florence's cheek one more time and dropped her hand, "Riley," she said as she took a breath and gave him a look of frustration. He said, "Florence Smith, one day the heavens will align, and we will have that kiss."

"Is that a promise Riley Simmons?" "You can count on it, sweetheart."

Jerry Smith was sitting on a stool at the Rattlesnake Bar Sunday afternoon drinking his beer and watching a rerun of an NFL game. He managed to get to the bar because he struck a deal with one of his stolen car buddies. He was going to be visiting one of his long-lost relatives, but just had to decide which one came first. He knew where his sister-in-law lived. He had lost track of the two little obnoxious kids. Well, Jerry guessed they weren't kids anymore.

He looked down at the bar and realized the peanut bowl was empty. He pushed the bowl towards the bartender and gestured for another beer.

Jerry eyed the TV and realized the game wasn't on and saw why. He scowled and said, "Damn commercials, waste of time and interrupting the damn game." Jerry watched as a commercial came on for a local theme park, "Damn waste of money paying to get into one of those places. Scam you out of your money and snot-nosed kids want every damn thing they see there." He glanced at the end of the bar to see some asshole staring at him, "Got a problem Mac?" The guy looked back at his beer.

"Yeah, I didn't think so," Jerry said. He started to take a swig of beer and his hand froze.

He got off his bar stool and looked closer. He saw a young woman dressed in cowgirl gear dancing in front of a float, "Well,

I'll be damned." He looked closer to make sure he was seeing what he thought he was seeing. The camera panned around and sure enough, there was a close up of his niece.

Jerry gave a salute with his beer towards the TV, "Well, hello there Florence. Nice to see you again." He sneered at the TV.

Jerry said in a sing-song voice, "Oh, Florence, you'll be hearing from me soon." He picked up the phone he had stolen and dialed the number.

When the person on the other end picked up, Jerry said, "Hey, I've got a little job for you.

I'll call you back with the details." Jerry hung up. He took a sip of beer and smiled.

Chapter 14

Sunday night, Riley was coming out of his bungalow to make his rounds.

"Hey man," Riley looked over and saw Hunt sitting on his stoop, "Hunt, what's up?"

"Just listening to the wonderful sounds of nothing. Hear how quiet it is? Crowds have all gone home so no kids screaming, no roller coasters climbing over the tracks again…and again…. and again." He let out a breath, looked at Riley and smiled.

"You do know that's my bread and butter you're talking about? I make a living having those crowds, hearing those kids screaming and listening to the coaster cars again…and again...and again. Come on Hunt. You love this park. Have you noticed where you live?"

"Yeah, I noticed," Hunt looked at his surroundings and then up at Riley, " You're right, I do love the park and think it's pretty cool to live in one, but I might be ready for a change."

Riley raised an eyebrow and sat down next to Hunt, "Well, I didn't see that coming." "Southern General Hospital has a job opening, head of Pediatrics."

He was stunned, "I didn't know you were looking."

"I wasn't. It kind of fell in my lap." Hunt leaned back on his elbows, "You remember Dr. Santos, right?"

"Yeah," Riley said, "He was our pediatrician when we were kids." "Well, he's finally retiring."

"Really?" Riley said, "I'll have to tell mom. He was a great doctor. I remember when mom went through her 'no sugar phase' with me. He used to sneak me those safety suckers.

Remember those---the round, flat suckers with the white wrap-around handle?" Hunt nodded and smiled.

Riley cleared his throat and continued his story, "Mom saw him give me one at my yearly checkup and she marched up to Doc and read him the riot act. Doc Santos said, "Now Mary, he's a growing boy and I know from what you've told me that his diet is 95% fruits, vegetables and healthy foods. You're a great mom. I love when parents take good care of their children, which you do. Coming to the doctor and getting a sucker twice a year, is that really something you want me to stop? If so, I will."

Mom looked at him relentlessly and huffed, "Fine, but only two a year. If anymore, I'll give Mrs. Santos a call and that will put an end to that." Riley and Hunt laughed, "I remember Doc agreeing with mom, winking at me, and sending me on my way. I hate to hear he's retiring, but that sounds like a good deal for you."

"He called me to see if I was interested in taking his spot. It would mean I'd still have to go before the hospital board, but he would recommend me. The board may have a problem with my age, in being so young, but Doc has followed my career. He liked what he saw and thought the hospital needed some young blood, so we'll see."

"So," Riley looked at Hunt and said, "Should I start looking for a new neighbor?"

Hunt said. “Let’s see what happens with the job first and how ‘bout I let you know?”

“Hmm,” he said, as he bumped Hunt’s shoulder, “You’ve been my best friend for as long as I can remember, I guess that will have to do.”

Riley stretched his legs out and they sat for a few minutes in companionable silence.

Hunt caught a motion out of the corner of his eye and elbowed his best friend, “Hey, is that Florence?”

Riley leaned forward. Yep, it was Florence. She was on the tail end of one of the trails that started at the Education Building. The trail backed up to one of the custodial buildings where all of the trash receptacles were stored. He wondered what she was doing back here. She never sought him out at home. Maybe this could be a step in the right direction.

Florence was late heading home. She wanted to do a little bit more planning in the building, but since it was a pretty night, thought she’d walk one of the trails. If she happened to run into Riley, then that would be the icing on the cake. She was a little nervous but was ready for a relationship with him. Florence continued walking, stretching her arms as she moved forward. As she got to the end of the trail, she heard voices and looked up.

The bungalows were up ahead. Hunt and Riley, feet planted on the stoop, gestured for her to join them. Florence headed in that direction but dropped her keys. Bending down to retrieve them pulled her attention away from the industrial trash receptacle barreling towards her from the storage area. She heard a shout and the sound of running. Florence felt the impact of the receptacle as metal hooks situated on the end tore through her blouse and shoulder and knocked her to the ground. The receptacle hit a wall and turned on its side, its wheels still spinning. When Riley reached Florence and saw the blood, his heart plummeted, “Florence!” yelled Riley.

Hunt ran to get his bag.

Florence looked up at Riley and winced. “Riley? What happened? Please help me!” Tears began to leak from her eyes, “Florence, honey, hang on. I’m right here. Let me see.” He looked at her shoulder.

Hunt came running, “Hang on Riley, you hold on to her.” As Riley held her, Hunt looked at the wound then at Florence, “All right hon, I’m going to have a look at your shoulder.” Hunt put on his medical gloves, cut the part of her blouse around the wound and applied direct pressure, “Okay, Riley, I need you to set your watch to 15 minutes.” Riley gazed at Hunt with a concerned expression and looked lost. Hunt tried again, “Riley, she’s going to be okay. It looks a lot worse than it is. Set your watch for 15 minutes.”

Riley nodded his head and set his watch. He watched the blood soak through the first cloth and glanced at Hunt. He covered the wound with a second cloth and continued to apply pressure. He looked up at Riley and watched as Riley gazed at Florence. Tears were streaming down her face.

He touched Florence’s cheek and said to her, “I’ve got you. It’s okay. Hunt’s here, and he isn’t going to let anything happen to you, are you Hunt?” Riley looked at Hunt.

He looked back at Riley and it started to click. Riley was in love with Florence.

Hunt tried for a little levity, “Florence, you’ll be healed and back at work in no time. Of course, I can’t do anything about you having to work for this guy.” Hunt glanced at him, “You know Florence, Riley and I have been best friends forever. He really has no sense of humor."

Riley tensed up when he saw Florence flinch in pain. Hunt continued to apply direct pressure as he talked, "Yes, I'm the funny one. Growing up in this theme park, I've heard a million theme park jokes. Here's one, "So a man is walking a penguin down the street on a leash. A policeman sees him and stops the man. The policeman says, "What are you doing? Take that penguin to the zoo." A week later, the policeman sees the man with the penguin again. He says, "Hey, I thought I told you to take that penguin to the zoo." The man replied, "I did! He loved it! Tomorrow we're going to the theme park!"

Riley's mouth quirked up and Florence just stared at Hunt, "Okay," Hunt said, "Tough crowd. Riley, she doesn't think I'm funny. Your turn."

"Florence," Riley lowered his voice as he held her, "One time I dated a girl who worked on the Tilt-a-Whirl. Our relationship didn't last long because everything had to revolve around her." Hunt chuckled and Riley heard a muffled sound from Florence.

Hunt looked at Riley and said, "Well Riley, I think that was a laugh from our patient here. Maybe you are funnier than me."

The sound of a timer going off had Riley raising his eyes to Hunt.

"Florence, listen to me hon. If Riley will lend us the use of his extra bathroom, we're going to carefully help you into his house."

Florence closed her eyes and took a deep breath.

Riley and Hunt gingerly helped Florence into Riley's bungalow. Reaching the bathroom, Hunt motioned for Florence to sit down in a chair, "I'm going to clean your wound and then

I'm putting in stitches. Sticking a bandage on it comes at the end. Ready?" Florence nodded.

"Riley, how 'bout you bring that stool by the door over and you can sit in front of Florence." With a stoic expression, Hunt continued, "I'm sorry Florence. You'll have to put up with looking at his face for the next few minutes."

Florence looked at Riley and his beautiful blue eyes and remarked, "Oh, I don't think I'll mind." Riley sent Hunt a smug smile, winked at Florence and held her hands. Hunt numbed the area and stitched her wound. A smile formed on Hunt's face as he gazed at Florence and Riley.

After Hunt finished stitching her shoulder, Florence called her mom and sister to explain what happened and to reassure them she was okay. By that time, an hour had passed, Riley handed her one of his button-down dress shirts and settled Florence in his extra bedroom.

She directed a tired smile at Hunt, "Thank you for everything."

"Not a problem. I'm going to leave some Tylenol here for pain, okay? Just be careful with those stitches." His last image of Florence was her drifting off to sleep. His mouth turned up.

Riley followed Hunt out of the room. Riley was the first to speak. He looked up at his best friend and clasped him on the shoulder, "Thank you."

"You're welcome. She should be fine. Now that everything has settled down with our Florence, I wanted to ask you what you thought about that receptacle flying out from nowhere."

Hunt watched Riley's expression transform from relief that Florence was okay to anger that someone would want to hurt her in his theme park, no less.

“I don’t know what to think,” Riley said, “I’ve never seen anyone be rude to her, have a problem with, or be angry with her since she’s been here. But you can bet I’ll be pulling videos tomorrow to see exactly what happened. Detective Drew Myers and I will have a discussion. I’m adding extra security tomorrow and will make sure every lock is double checked. No one is going to wreak havoc in this park.”

“I’ll keep a look out as well,” Hunt spied the other bungalows, “I didn’t see Aunt Alice when I pulled in this evening. She okay?”

“Yes,” Riley answered,” She’s staying with Elmira tonight. Something about a girl’s night?”

Hunt chuckled, “Good for them.” Hunt put his hands in his pockets and lingered at Riley’s door.

“Something on your mind?” Riley shifted in his stance and looked at Hunt with worry in his eyes, “Is something wrong with Florence you're not telling me?”

Hunt’s affect was somber as he glanced at Riley. He cleared his throat, “When stitching her up, I noticed faint circular scars on her back.”

Riley’s expression showed confusion, “I don’t understand.”

Hunt continued his explanation, “Riley, when I worked in the ER, these marks were very common.” Riley put his hands on his hips and waited.

“Cigarette burns. At some time in her life, she was burned with a cigarette.”

Chapter 15

Riley sat in the rocking chair in Florence's room and couldn't clear his mind of the image of Florence being burned with cigarettes. At first, Riley had been horrified because, who does that? Then, he felt sadness for Florence. Now a slow anger was building. As he watched her sleep, he wanted to ask her what happened. Then he wanted to find the SOB and beat the living daylights out of him. That wasn't really his style, but what kind of asshole burns someone with cigarettes, especially if she was a little girl when it happened.

Then, Riley thought about that trash receptacle hitting Florence. Earlier after he checked to make sure she was still asleep he called his friend, the detective. Drew had arrived earlier and inspected the receptacle. He asked Riley if the hooks that tore into Florence's shoulder were standard hooks on that receptacle. He emphasized his answer with a shake of his head. Drew then took pictures for evidence and even dusted for prints. Wearing gloves, the detective moved the receptacle into a private storage place for safe keeping. Drew told Riley he would be in touch.

As he rocked in the chair and watched Florence, he was distressed that he hadn't been fast enough to stop her from getting hit. What if the hooks had hit her eyes or caused a head injury when she hit the ground? He could play "what if" all night long.

He leaned over to smooth her hair back from her face and she stirred. Riley kissed the top of her head. After a minute or two she settled back down.

He sat back and let the peaceful movement of the rocking chair lull him to sleep. Riley woke a few hours later to sounds of thrashing coming from the bed. It registered with him that it was Florence tossing and turning. She finally cried out and sat straight up in the bed and looked around, confused.

Riley moved to the side of the bed,"Hey there, it's okay. I'm right here." Florence glanced at Riley and he asked, "Want to talk about it?"

Florence shook her head adamantly, "It was a nightmare. I've had it before, but it's been several years. I don't know why it chose tonight to come back and haunt me." Florence moved slightly and grimaced.

Riley walked away only to return with a glass of water and two pills. "Here," Riley said, "These may help."

After Florence had her fill of water, she handed the glass back to him, "Thank you." She hugged her knees to her chest.

Riley hated the fear showing in her eyes, "Do you think you can go back to sleep?"

Her hands trembled and she uttered, "I don't want to stay in this bed. I don't want to have another nightmare like that again tonight."

His heart was breaking for her, "Florence, do you trust me?" asked Riley. "Of course I do," said Florence,

"Okay, then let's try something." Riley picked her up from the bed and carried her with him to sit on his lap in the rocking chair. Once she was settled on his lap, she put her head on his chest and began to sob. His heart shattered all over again and he held her.

When the sobs turned into tears, and the tears subsided, Riley just held on to her. He smoothed her hair away from her face and began to rock, "Florence, can you tell me about the cigarette burns on your back?" He could feel Florence flinch, but he held on, letting the sway of the chair lull her into feeling comfortable enough to tell him her story.

Florence burrowed further into Riley's chest and began to talk, "When my father died, we didn't have anywhere to go, so we moved in with my uncle on my father's side of the family. He was not very nice, and we learned pretty quickly to stay out of his way. Since I was older than Karen, I tried to deflect his attention away from her to me. He was verbally abusive to us girls, but he knocked our mother down if she talked back to him." Riley closed his eyes and held Florence a little tighter. "Mom used to tell him not to smoke in the house and he just cursed at her. One day, I just got fed up with his cursing and smoking. So, when I knew he was out of the house, I threw his cigarettes in the garbage. When he got home, he was yelling at my mom and I didn't want him to hit her, so I confessed to throwing out his cigarettes. He ranted and cursed at me and told me never to touch anything of his again. I thought that was the end of it. But that night when everyone went to sleep, I got up to get some water and...and..."

Florence's tears were running down her face as she raised her eyes to glance at Riley. He wiped the tears away, "Florence, you don't have to finish." She raised her hand to his cheek. He was such a kind man. She shook her head as though to clear the horror out of her mind.

"He cornered me in the kitchen. He covered my mouth so

no one would hear me screaming, pulled the back of my pajama top down and burned me with his cigarette, not once, but three times. He told me if I ever breathed a word of what he had done to my teachers at school or anyone for that matter, he would hurt my mom and Karen." She cringed and covered her eyes with her hands, "Then he said he'd come after me."

As Florence finished her story, she realized the chair had stopped moving.

She raised her head and saw tears streaming down Riley's face. "Oh, Riley!" She touched his cheek, and he kissed the palm of her hand through his tears.

Riley couldn't find anywhere for his anger to go and didn't want Florence to think anything was directed at her, "What a horrible life," he thought. Riley shifted in the chair, cleared his throat, and asked, "What happened to your uncle?"

Florence answered, "Well, after about a year of living with our uncle, a new neighbor moved in next door. He was a nice man. His name is Edward. We found out he lost his daughter and wife in a car crash. Their car hydroplaned in the rain and they were killed instantly. He kept somc of his daughter's things because he was waiting for the right time to let them go and offered us her toys. He told us she would be very happy to know her toys would be loved by other little girls. Edward kind of took us under his wings and figured out what was going on with our uncle. He conferred with his supervisor and the Department of Human Resources.

"You see, Edward was a policeman. That's how he picked up on the signs that we were being abused." Florence took a big breath and continued speaking, "My uncle was arrested and has been in jail for 18 years. The judge at the time gave mom the house as compensation for the abuse. Our neighbor, Edward, has since retired from the police department. He made a deal with a detective to let us know whenever my uncle is up for parole. Edward and I go before the Parole Board and ask that due to the abuse we suffered, that he remain in jail. So far, he's still there."

Florence remained quiet and had nothing more to say on the matter.

Riley continued to rock Florence in the chair. Florence asked if they could turn on soft music. Songs of love filled the air. Riley was content to hold Florence and said nothing more. After a while, he knew it was time, "Florence," Riley said, "Can I ask you a question?"

Florence raised her head and looked at Riley.

He found the courage to speak, "Who is Curtis Dalton and what does he mean to you?"

Florence put her head back on Riley's chest, "Curtis is the older brother of the man who was my fiancé." Riley stopped the chair and lifted Florence's chin, "Your fiancé?"

"Yes, Riley. Three years ago, I had a fiancé named Keith. Curtis is his brother."

"Where is Keith now?" asked Riley. Florence took a deep breath and looked at him, "He's dead." Riley didn't know what to say.

Florence began to talk, "I met Keith in college. His sister, Leslie, was my classmate. Keith and I would cross paths when his sister would bring me to visit their farm. We started dating. His family has a big farm in Baldwin County, and I used to hang around there a lot learning about the animals, crops and life on a farm."

Riley interrupted, "So, when I took you to the Founding Farmer's section and you cried, Keith was the reason why."

"Yes," Florence said, "I was heartbroken that he never got to live out his dream. You see, it was his dream to run the family farm. That's all he ever wanted to do. Well, farm and…"

"Marry you," added Riley.

Florence nodded, "He asked me to marry him and I said yes. I just knew we would have a happy life."

Riley waited for her to continue, "Before we were to be married, Keith was coming home from an Agriculture Conference and was hit head on by a drunk driver. He was killed on impact and the driver of the other car walked away without a scratch." Florence stared at Riley.

"I was so sad and angry for such a long time. His family was so good to me. They continued to reach out to let me know that I was still part of their family." Tears welled up in her eyes,

"Of course, I couldn't go back to the farm. I just couldn't. The pain was just too much."

She laid her head on Riley's chest. He didn't speak, so Florence continued talking to him about Keith, "I felt bad for the longest time because they were so kind to me and I let them down by not going back to the farm. Of course, Curtis told me they understood."

Her eyes met Riley's, "Curtis checks on me, especially around the anniversary of Keith's death."

Riley held his breath, "Florence," he asked, "how do you feel about Curtis?"

She quietly answered, "I love him." Riley closed his eyes and felt everything fall apart.

Florence spoke up again, "He's like the brother I never had."

Riley let out a long, slow breath, "I was a real jerk to him yesterday when we met. He's important to you and now I understand why. I'm so sorry."

"Yes," Florence said, "After we left you and your mom, he had us stop to sit down in the park so he could talk to me. He said he knew why you acted the way you did."

"He did, huh?" Riley said.

"He wanted to make sure you understood that he wasn't replacing his brother. Curtis loves me as a sister and a friend and nothing more."

Riley thought about that, "Why would he want me to know that?"

"Here we go," thought Florence, "He wanted you to know that because he figured it out." Riley's heart was thumping in his chest, "Figured out what?"

Florence raised her head, looked Riley straight in the eye and said, "He figured out you were the one. Curtis said you were the one who was going to take away all my sorrow and pain. You, Riley, are the one."

"Am I now?"

"Yes, Riley," Florence said, as she moved her hands up his chest and held his face. Then she kissed him. All the frustration, all the feelings he had for her, all of the misunderstandings, poured into this kiss. Florence deepened the kiss and he responded passionately.

Riley went to touch her shoulders and she flinched. "Florence, Oh, Florence, I'm so sorry."

"It's okay, it's still tender." She looked at him and smiled. "We can't seem to catch a break, can we?"

He breathed her name as he kissed her forehead, her nose

and then her mouth. "I have an idea." He looked at the bed. Florence raised an eyebrow. Riley stood up with her in his arms.

"Hold on to me." She held on to him as he picked her up.

Florence held his eyes with hers and said breathlessly, "Now what do we do?"

Riley gave her a slow smile and kissed her, "Now, Florence, we dance." They moved around the room and had eyes only for each other. The soft music continued to play in the background.

"Two less lonely people in the world and it's going to be fine. Out of all the people in the world, I just can't believe your mine". They continued to move to the music.

Florence asked Riley to put her down. Riley released her. As her feet touched the ground, Florence murmured, "I don't know how to begin."

"Just talk to me. I'm not going anywhere."

She nervously glanced at him, "I've never had relations with a man before." She blew out a big breath.

He stared at her, "Florence, you were engaged at one time."

She told him when she was engaged, she was ready to give herself completely to Keith, but he wanted their first time to be special, so they waited, "It wasn't due to lack of trying. We almost compromised ourselves, but he was serious about waiting until our wedding night."

Riley picked up her hand and kissed it, "Thank you for telling me." "Riley?"

His eyes met hers, "Yes, Florence?"

She twisted her hands together. He stepped forward and held her hands. Florence swallowed, "I'd like to be with you tonight."

Riley gazed at Florence. He kissed her forehead. His mouth touched her mouth. His eyes met hers. He tenderly touched her cheek.

Morning came early as daylight peaked through the curtains of Riley's bedroom.

He looked over at Florence, who was still sleeping soundly. He hated to wake her. He just wanted a few minutes to look at her. They were finally together. He realized what a gift she had given him. He realized he just didn't want to be the first. He wanted to be the only. He sighed and heard a noise coming from his dresser next to the bed. Riley took one last look at Florence. He realized the noise was coming from his phone. He received a text from Hunt, "If you tore those stitches last night, I'm going to kick your ass!" Riley continued reading, "If nothing happened last night to cause those stitches to be torn, then I'll apologize. If something did happen last night, I'm happy for you two. You're good together and I really like Florence. She classes up the joint."

Hunt then texted, "I'll be there at 6:45 AM sharp to look at Florence's shoulder. Please make yourselves presentable. P.S.-- I'm bringing apple and pumpkin muffins from Aunt Alice.... that is if I don't eat them first!"

Riley smiled. He was really going to miss Hunt if he got that job. But he'd be happy for him, he thought, as he turned back towards Florence. Her eyes were wide open, and she was looking at him. She gave Riley a slow smile and he smiled right back at her. He leaned over and said, "Miss Smith, are you lost?"

Florence met him halfway, kissed him and answered, "No, Mr. Simmons, I'm right where I need to be."

"That's good to know," Riley replied, as his lips touched

hers. He started to deepen the kiss then remembered Hunt, "Florence, we're about to have company. In about 30 minutes Dr. George Huntington will be walking through that door with a basket of muffins and a medical bag." Florence gave Riley a smoldering look, "Race you to the shower."

Riley and Florence were sitting at the table in the kitchen eating muffins and drinking coffee when Hunt walked out of the bathroom rolling his shirtsleeves down.

"Well, Florence, the stitches looked good and the area around the wound is clean. For the life of me, though, I don't know why the bandage was so damp." He looked at Riley and Florence, who were concentrating very hard on drinking their coffee and not looking at him.

Hunt joined them both at the table, reached for a muffin and slathered it with butter.

He looked up to see Florence and Riley staring at him, "What?" he asked, as he munched on his muffin.

Riley looked down at Hunt's muffin and asked, "As a doctor aren't you supposed to be walking the walk and talking the talk when it comes to eating healthy?"

Hunt looked in the middle of the table at the basket of fruit. He pulled out a banana and held it up to Riley, "Satisfied?" As Hunt started to peel the banana, he said, "Ok, Florence, I'm going to try this one more time, so I can redeem myself from apparently my pitiful attempt at humor last night. Why did the banana go to the doctor? Because it wasn't peeling well."

There was silence at the table. "Crickets," he muttered, "I'm only hearing crickets," said Hunt as he cleared his place, grabbed his coat and bag, and walked out the front door.

Florence and Riley covered their faces with their hands and

burst out laughing.

Riley was still shaking from laughter when he said, “God love him, I hope at least his patients laugh when he tells those jokes.”

“What kind of doctor is he? “asked Florence as she took a sip of her coffee.

“Pediatrician,” Riley said, then winked at Florence, who almost choked on her coffee.

Chapter 16

Florence couldn't return to work until the end of the week, so she was a little apprehensive, but glad when she was finally able to walk through the employee gate to start her day. Florence wasn't one to sit and do nothing, so the week of the confinement was not one of her finest times. Of course, carving out time for her and Riley to be together had been her favorite part of the week. He had even managed to get Toni to cover for him so he could take her to lunch. They had picked up Riley's mom on the way to the restaurant in Pensacola so she could join them. The restaurant was situated on the bay, it had been a gorgeous day and the view was terrific.

Florence thought she would feel awkward around Mrs. Simmons now that she and Riley were together, but his mom had greeted her with a hug and had chatted with them all through lunch. Over a lunch of seafood baskets, she had shared stories about Riley as a young boy and some of the mischief he used to get himself into. Mary Simmons talked at length about the time he had scooped up all the neighbors' newspapers, spread them out on the sidewalk, and took off on his bike. When he got close to the newspaper, Riley would hit the brakes, causing his bike to fishtail and slide on the newspapers. Riley said the newspapers made for great traction.

Sitting at the table in the warm sunshine, they all shared a laugh.

Riley's mom continued, saying that it wasn't so funny when one of the neighbors came to her door to tell her what Riley had done, and it wasn't so funny when his dad got home. His dad made Riley take money out of his savings jar he kept in his room and then he took Riley to the store to buy newspapers to replace the ones he had taken from the neighbors' sidewalks. Then they went door to door so Riley could apologize and hand each neighbor a new paper.

His mom winked at Riley and told them that was the last time Riley did something like that.

Riley told Florence that the paper episode came back to haunt him when he got a job cutting the neighbors' yards. They'd see Riley coming with his lawnmower and run out to get their papers before he reached their yard. Florence and Mary broke into laughter with Riley rolling his eyes and shaking his head.

Florence had never laughed this much in a long time. She liked Riley's mom. When they dropped her off after lunch that day, she hugged Florence and kissed Riley. Riley later shared with Florence that his mom was glad she was in his life.

Florence swiped her Employee ID and walked into the Education building. She waited by the front door as she turned the lights on. Now that she was back in the park, she felt on edge.

She had noticed that there were extra security guards monitoring the park. She remembered Riley was all about his guests and employees feeling safe in the park.

She thought back when Riley had finally broached the subject of that night.

Riley had told her he had viewed the footage from the cameras.

There had been what appeared to be a man running and jumping over a privacy fence and then nothing. Riley had Rafael from the Tech Department view it as well, but when he couldn't come to a conclusion, Riley had sent it to his police contact, Drew Myers. Drew had wanted to meet with Riley, Hunt and Florence. The meeting was scheduled for this afternoon in the park conference room. Florence looked around the front lobby. It was too quiet in here.

She made her way to the nearest classroom where she had left her plans for the week. She heard a noise and stopped mid-stride. She saw the door was open. It was mandatory that all doors are locked at night in every building. She didn't have anything to protect herself but her keys. She grabbed the longest key and slid it between two fingers as she inched sideways in the hallway and carefully peaked through the door.

There was a man in the classroom that was standing with his back to her. He had short blond hair and was wearing a red shirt and khakis. He held a black object in his hand. Florence moved her hand along the door, which caused the door to swing open even further and bang the wall behind the door.

The man with the blonde hair swung around with the black object still in his hand.

Florence turned to run, but stopped when she heard the man say, "Miss Smith?"

Florence turned around and recognized the young man in the park uniform and breathed a sigh of relief, "Kevin?"

"Yes ma'am," Then he said to Florence, "Miss Smith, are you okay? If you don't mind me saying so, you look very pale."

Florence walked into the room and put her bag on the desk. She looked at the young man whom Riley had given the chance to be a tech assistant at the park. He had cut his hair short and had only one earring. His hair no longer covered his face.

"Kevin," Florence exclaimed, "you startled me!"

"I'm sorry, Miss Smith. I was told to install the new smartboard that was ordered for the classroom."

Florence now looked closer and realized Kevin had a controller in his hand. She let out a small breath and asked, "How come the lights in the lobby weren't turned on when you walked into the building?"

"Oh, Miss Smith," Kevin answered, "I'm sorry about that. It's calming without the lights on. I'm so used to having my lights off at home when working on my computer. I guess I just didn't think to turn them on."

He looked so stricken that Florence waved her hand in the air, "Not a problem. If you would please remember to turn them on next time, I would really appreciate it."

"Sure thing, Miss Smith," Kevin said, as he looked at Ms. Smith and tapped his foot. He looked at the smartboard.

"Oh, Kevin, don't mind me. I just came to get my plans."

"Yes, ma'am," Kevin turned back to his work. Florence got her plans off her desk, stored them in her bag, and told Kevin goodbye.

As Florence was walking out of the lobby, her bag slipped off her arm. As she put it back on, she bumped into a man and almost screamed.

"Riley!" Florence dropped her bag and gave Riley a big hug and hung on. "Florence, what happened?" he asked, as he held her tight.

She let out a big breath and then looked at Riley, with those beautiful blue eyes and the comforting hugs. She eased back from his arms, "Oh, nothing, it's nothing." She shook her head. He looked at her and waited. Florence said, "Really, Riley, I just got spooked. I went inside to get my plans and got startled when Kevin was there working on the smartboard. I just didn't expect anyone to be there, that's all. I think having that meeting on my mind and having to talk to the detective has just been a little unnerving for me today."

He started to speak, but Florence put her hands on his chest, "I'll be fine. Really."

He gave her a worried look, took the palm of one hand and kissed it. Her breath caught in her throat. Continuing to gaze into her eyes, Riley took the other hand and kissed her palm.

Florence sighed, "You really know how to make me feel better." He gave her one of his slow, sexy smiles.

She smiled, "I see you don't disagree."

He picked up her bag and handed it to her. They began to walk towards the front door and Riley remarked, "I wouldn't dare disagree with a woman who is so much smarter than me."

Chapter 17

Riley and Florence reached the main offices at the front of the park before the meeting with Detective Myers.

Riley stuck his head into Toni's office. She was visiting with her daughter Tori. Riley moved further into the room and hugged her, "Tori, it's good to see you again. Have you seen Scott and his dad lately?"

Tori gazed at Riley. He sure was a good-looking man. If not for the woman standing in the doorway looking at him with love in her eyes, Tori could see herself being interested in a date with Riley. Oh, who was she kidding, he was like a brother to her. She had known him forever and couldn't imagine being romantic with him. She grinned.

Riley saw her grinning and asked her what was so funny.

Her eyes sparkled and she shook her head, "Nothing important. You asked if I have seen Scott and Jacob? Yes, they came into the center earlier this week. One of our teachers worked on social skills with Scott while I met with his dad. He's a nice man who's had a rough go of it," Tori didn't say anything else and seemed to be lost in thought. Riley noticed and shared a look with Toni.

"You have your meeting in a few minutes with the

detective?" asked Toni.

Florence walked further into the room with a nervous expression on her face. Riley put his arm around her. Toni looked at Riley and smiled. She was glad the two of them had finally realized they should be together. It was nice to see.

Riley's eyes met Toni's and his mouth curved, "Yes. Are you going to be here in the office or are you all headed out?"

Toni spoke up, "If you can spare me, I would like to introduce Tori to our new coffee shop, the French Press."

"Mom has told me so much about it." Tori glanced at Riley, "You know what a fan of caffeine I can be. I can't wait." Riley told Toni he had his radio with him and to have a nice visit.

Detective Drew Myers was very trendy in a green Havana suit with a white and tan striped polo. He was about 6'2" and very fit. He had ebony skin and a close-cropped head of hair. Riley had known Drew for several years now. He had at one time advised his uncle about the security of the park, and they were better off now for taking that advice.

Florence, Riley, and Hunt were all seated around the table in the conference room in the main office area. To his credit the detective wasn't fazed by the custom-made chairs each depicting an animal found on a carousel. Florence had signed her contract to work in the park in this very room. She was told at that time that when Uncle Frank and Riley's dad had gone on a business trip to New Orleans, they happened to stop by a famous bar at one of the hotels.

The bar slowly turned in a circle and had chairs representing animals found on a carousel. As the story goes, his dad and uncle found a seat. As they sipped their Old Fashioneds at the revolving bar, they looked at each other and smiled, the idea hitting them both at once.

When they got back to the park, they had the chairs custom made and installed in the front conference room. Florence had chosen the zebra chair as she liked it the best. She needed the comfort to get through the next 30 minutes.

Detective Myers looked around the room. "Everyone ready?" Riley nodded.

Detective Myers opened his notebook, "On Sunday evening, September 18th at approximately 9 PM, Florence Smith, park educator, was taking a walk on one of the trails in the park." The detective nodded towards Florence and continued, "You, Miss Smith, heard noises and realized it was Dr. George Huntington and Riley Simmons on their front porch. You began to walk their way and happened to drop your keys. When picking them up, you were hit by an industrial trash receptacle and injured."

Detective Myers looked at Hunt and Riley. "Dr. Huntington and Mr. Simmons came to your aid in which Dr. Huntington took care of your wound with Mr. Simmons assisting the doctor." The detective continued, "There is a video that identifies what we see is a man in a hat jumping over the privacy fence and running away. Currently our department is working on enhancing the video to identify what we believe to be the suspect in question, then we will be looking at our extensive database of those with criminal records, fingerprints on file, etc.

In gathering data, it was concluded that a main lock to the receptacle area was broken off with a pair of bolt cutters and that is how the suspect accessed the receptacle which injured Miss Smith." Detective Myers asked if anyone at the table saw anything out of the ordinary,

"Anything would help. Think of people that were lingering in the park, looked out of place or anything unusual that may have happened." The detective looked in Florence's direction.

Florence looked at Riley and Hunt then shook her head. Florence exclaimed, "Detective Myers, I didn't see anything until I got hit. I was walking the trail. I didn't see anyone following me. The first people I saw were Riley and Hunt."

"Miss Smith," asked the detective, "do you know of any reason someone would want to harm you? Did you have an argument with anyone recently?"

Florence shook her head.

"Okay," said Detective Myers, "Anything in your past that would lead you to believe that someone would want to harm you?"

Florence sat very still and slowly put her hand over Riley's hand under the table. She couldn't speak.

Detective Myers paused, "Miss Smith, I know this is difficult, but I need an answer please."

Florence squeezed Riley's hand. Riley spoke up, "Drew, I think that's it for now." Riley looked at Hunt, "Hunt, do you have anything else to add?"

Hunt shook his head, looked at Riley and replied, "No, I don't have anything to add."

The detective's perceptive eyes gazed at Florence, then Riley, and then Hunt. His eyes traced back to Florence. He began to speak, "Folks, this is not helping anyone. If there is something I need to know I need to know it now if I am going to have any chance of solving this case and keeping Miss Smith safe." He was met with a wall of silence.

Detective Myers closed his notebook and stood up.

The detective nodded at Florence, "Well, when you are ready to tell me anything else, here's my card." The detective slid the card on the table towards Florence and said, "I will be in touch, thank you."

Riley, Florence, and Hunt waited until the door closed. Florence then let the tears flow and held on to Riley, "I can't do it Riley. I don't want to go through explaining what happened to me and my family with the detective."

Riley wiped her tears and said, "Florence, you are one of the strongest people I have ever met. If there is any chance that your uncle is somehow connected to this, you need to talk to Drew. Maybe you're not as safe as you think. I can't take the chance of you getting hurt again. I barely made it through the first time."

Florence looked at Riley, then at Hunt, "Hunt, I…". Florence tried to explain. Hunt put his hand over hers, looked at her and said, "I know."

Florence looked at Riley. Hunt squeezed her hand, "I saw the marks when I cleaned your shoulder."

Her tears began to flow again. Riley took her in his arms and kissed the top of her head. "You don't have to do this alone. There are a lot of people here at this park who care about you."

Florence gasped, "Oh, my God, Riley, the park! I can't be here anymore. I can't risk anyone getting hurt because of me. If my injury wasn't an accident, then he knows I'm here." Florence cried and said, "Riley, I just found you. I don't want to lose you." She clung to him. "Hon, I'm not going to let that happen. Look at me." He tipped her face up to his. He kissed her then held her in his arms, "I'm here. As long as it's in my power, I'm always going to be here for you." Riley looked at Hunt and he nodded, "Between the three of us here, you, me, and Hunt…. we can figure this out."

Florence looked at them. Florence wiped her eyes and said, "Like the Three Amigos." Riley smiled and said, "The Three Musketeers" and glanced at Hunt.

Hunt smiled and shrugged, “The Three Stooges?”

Florence and Riley stared at Hunt and laughed. Hunt winked at them and remarked, “It’s about time someone laughed at my jokes. I don’t get it. I’m a funny guy!”

Riley grinned and shook his head at his best friend. “Well, it happens!” They all chuckled.

Hunt looked at his watch, “I hate to leave good company, but I have to get some shut eye because I have a late shift.” He stood up and took her hand, “It’s all going to be okay.”

He focused his gaze on Riley and offered, “Believe it or not, he’s a good guy to have in your corner.” Riley put his hand on Hunt’s shoulder and Florence smiled. Hunt waved and left the room.

Riley observed her wipe her eyes, “Florence, I’d like to take you somewhere tonight where you can relax and feel some peace. How ‘bout it?” She nodded her head and hugged him. “That sounds wonderful, Riley. Thank you.”

That evening, Florence was lying on her stomach in a hammock watching the calmness of the bay and listening to a soothing playlist she had programmed on her phone. Riley had driven her to a friend’s house situated on the water in Point Clear. The friend was out of town but had given Riley a key a long time ago just in case he ever needed to get away. Riley was sitting on the steps leading down to the crab wharf. The hammock was tucked into the corner of the pier, but Florence had a wonderful view. She took a calming breath, “Riley, this is heaven.

I’ll have to write your friend a nice thank you note. The dinner you made was wonderful as well.” Riley glanced at the table behind them at the fast-food bags filled with empty burger wrappers and french fry boxes. He grinned, “Yes, Florence

Smith, it took me all of 10 minutes to prepare that meal for you. Maybe one night, you can return the favor." He eyed the hammock and gazed at Florence, "You think that can hold both of us?" Florence eyed his body from head to toe, "Hmm, I better come to you." His eyes expressed his desire. She walked down the steps and sat in front of him. He pulled her into his body and rested his arms over her shoulders. Riley kissed her on the top of her head. They gazed out at the water.

It was a magical night. She leaned back into Riley's arms and closed her eyes. Riley began to massage her shoulders, "That feels so good." He worked his hands down her back. He took a breath and continued his journey up to her neck, "Florence?"

She was trying to catch her breath, "Yes, Riley?" He cupped her shoulders,

"Do you think we can take this inside?"

She turned around and met his gaze, "I thought you'd never ask." Florence and Riley cleaned up and turned out the lights to the pier. Riley opened the screened door that led into the back porch and Florence walked ahead of him. He then took her hand and led her to the guest bedroom upstairs. Riley opened the windows and the breeze off the bay caused the sheer white curtains to flutter. Riley thought she was so beautiful. He walked towards her and took her hand. He kissed it and hugged her to him. She rubbed her hands down his back.

He kissed her cheek. Florence touched her mouth to his. He pulled her to his chest. As the sensations of love swirled around them, the wind picked up outside the windows, in preparation for the approaching storm.

Jerry Smith was parked down the block from his sister-in-law's house, or correction, his house. Looks like someone had decided to fix up the old neighborhood. Fixer-uppers had been torn down and rebuilt. He saw people walking their dogs and young couples out jogging and parents pushing a baby stroller. Damn yuppies, he thought. Nothing wrong with the way the old neighborhood was back in the day. As he looked back at the house, he was thinking. Jerry had to figure out how to get into the house.

He'd been watching Janet's routine, so he knew when she wouldn't be home. But he had to watch the cop come and go from his house. It looked like he hung around, but he had to leave his house sometime. Jerry couldn't have that nosy cop around while he tried to take care of business. His buddy had done a good job with the niece at that park. She had no reason to suspect him because as far as she knew, he was in jail. He was ready to get his money and move the hell on. No way was he going to waste his time checking in with some damn parole officer. Tomorrow, he would begin what he liked to call Operation Payback.

He rolled down the window, threw out the cigarette he'd been smoking, and whistled as he drove away

Chapter 18

Florence had a lot of time to think about her meeting she had with Riley and Hunt that day in the conference room at the park. She had loved her time of peace at the bay with him. She realized she really did have many people who cared about her: Riley and his family, Hunt, her family, and the Daltons. She had made friends at the park as well, not to mention really enjoying her job. Florence understood Riley and Hunt wanted to help, but she needed to put an end to what was happening. Riley wouldn't be happy, but if she was going to have any chance of a life with him, she needed to do this on her own terms. That meant going back to where it all started.

She got out of her car and took in the freshly painted house, new windows, a well-kept yard, and new railings on the steps. She took a deep breath and rang the bell. When the door opened, Florence looked at the lady with the brown hair piled on top of her head, petite figure and intelligent green eyes that were filled with sorrow. She stepped into the house right into her mom's arms.

Florence hugged her mom and tears started to flow down her face, "Oh, mom," Florence cried, "I thought we were through with all this."

Janet hugged her daughter, "We got through it then and

we're going to get through it now, together." Her mom gazed at everyone in the room. Florence spotted Edward. He enveloped her in a big bear hug. He always reminded Florence of the actor, Brian Dennehy. Edward was big, strong and you could always count on him to fix everything.

Karen came up to them and put her hand on Florence's shoulder, "We've come too far, this family. Flo, are you ready?" Florence looked at all of them, "Yes, let's go."

Karen walked with her sister out of the house as their mom and Edward walked behind them. Karen looked at Florence and asked, "Riley? He's not coming with us?" Karen knew that they were in a relationship.

"No. I don't want him getting hurt over something that happened in our family."

Karen stopped and grabbed her arm, "Flo, I know he loves you, even if he hasn't said it to you yet. Don't you think he'd want to support you? Won't he be hurt if you don't include him?"

"I know you mean well, but this is something I've thought about for a long time and this is the only way." As Florence drove them all to the police station to meet with Detective Myers, she thought about her family in the car. She was so glad the family she loved was still with her.

Riley Simmons prided himself on being easy going but focused on what he wanted out of life. He always felt those qualities were what made him so successful at running the park and getting along with people he met, at least most of the time. So, when Drew Myers had called to confirm the time for the meeting Florence had set up at the police station, that easy going, focused person was nowhere to be found.

As Riley drove to the police station, he was confused and

hurt. Weren't he and Florence doing well in their relationship? He knew he hadn't said the words, but Florence had to know his feelings. She was everything to him. He pulled into the police station, and he wanted her to know how much he cared about her.

Florence, her mom, Edward, and Karen were shown into a large conference room at the police station. The conference room had a mini fridge filled with water bottles and a coffee machine.

Detective Drew Myers was not alone when he walked into the conference room.

Riley was with him. Florence had a look of surprise on her face.

Riley zeroed in on Florence with a look of disappointment. He sat down across the table from her. Florence was disappointed as well. She thought the way she had handled things had been for the best. She soaked up the sight of him. Yes, she loved Riley. She loved him with all her heart. Just because she hadn't said it yet didn't make it any less true. She looked up at Riley and he looked at the detective. Tears started to form in her eyes, and she blinked them away.

Detective Myers took a seat by Riley and placed a notebook and file folder on the table.

He read from his notes, "We are meeting today at 3:00 PM. Present in the room are Riley Simmons, Florence Smith, Janet Smith, Karen Smith and Edward Howard. Dr. George Huntington is not attending due to an emergency at the hospital.

This is a meeting to discuss further information on the injury of Florence Smith on the night she was hit by an industrial trash receptacle on the grounds of the Jubilee Sunset Theme Park. The injury was to the shoulder and recovery completed with a return recently to her job at the theme park."

Florence looked at Riley. His eyes were downcast staring at the table with his hands folded.

The detective then continued with further information: "There was a meeting prior to this one at the theme park conference room with Dr. George Huntington, Riley Simmons and Florence Smith. The sequence of events leading up to Miss Smith's injury and possible motives to cause her harm were discussed and considered inconclusive with the questioning of Miss Smith.

Mr. Simmons provided a video of a man jumping over a privacy fence away from the park. At the time of the meeting, further information on the alleged suspect was not yet completed nor provided." The detective stared at Florence.

"Miss Smith, I have reason to believe in the prior meeting you were holding back information that would help us proceed with this case. Frankly, I was surprised when you called me." Florence looked at the detective, "Would you like to explain to me, please, why you called me?"

Florence looked at Riley who was staring back at her. Well, she thought, at least he's looking at me now. Florence cleared her throat and said, "Well, when I was about 12 years old," She looked at Karen. "our father died. He drank himself to death." Janet Smith shifted in her seat and folded her hands on the table. Edward covered her hand. "We didn't have anywhere to go, so my mom, Karen and myself moved in with our Uncle, Jerry Smith. He was abusive to us. He would knock mom down if she talked back to him and he was verbally abusive to Karen." Tears filled Florence's eyes and flowed down her cheeks. There was a box of Kleenex on the table that Riley pushed across the table to her. She looked up at him. He nodded his head for her to continue her story. She dabbed her eyes with a Kleenex and explained, "He used to smoke in the house when mom asked him not to and I was sick of him hitting mom and treating us that way.

One night when he was out, I threw his cigarettes in the trash. When he came home, he was livid. He was yelling at mom and about to hit her, so I told him I threw his cigarettes in the trash. He told me not to touch his things ever again, and I thought that was the end of that." She took a deep breath and looked around the room. Her mom and Karen both had tears in their eyes and Edward was holding her mom. She peeked at Riley and saw their future in his eyes. His eyes were shining with love.

She smiled at him through her tears and that gave her the courage to continue.

Florence looked at the detective and said, "I woke up that night and needed a drink of water. So, I went into the kitchen, filled up a glass with water and turned around. He was there. My uncle was standing behind me, and he looked very angry. He was smoking a cigarette. He grabbed the glass from me and set it on the counter."

Florence started crying. Riley couldn't stand it any longer. He walked around the table to comfort his love, "Riley," she cried. "Riley!" Riley held on to her while she cried. Her mother and Karen came to hug her as well.

As Riley held on to Florence tightly, Janet Smith looked at him and said through her tears, "I want to thank you for being there for Florence." Riley nodded.

Janet looked at her daughters and said, "Girls, I'm so sorry. I've always felt it was all my fault. I didn't know where to turn and I wanted you to have a home. We should've left and gone into a shelter, but I was so afraid for all of us," She continued crying.

Edward came to hold her. Janet looked at Edward and told him, “You saved us. I’m so sorry we wasted all of those years. I was letting my past ruin my future.” He hugged her.

Florence said, “Mom, you were as much a victim as we were. You thought we would be a family there, but Uncle Jerry didn’t care about anyone but himself.”

Karen added, “Mom, we had each other, and we came out stronger for it. He can’t take that away from us. We love you.”

Detective Myers looked up from his notes and said to Florence, “You have your family with you. You’ve come this far.” He looked around the room at everyone, “You’re very fortunate that you have each other.” He looked at Florence, “How about taking that next step and finishing it?”

With Riley still holding her and surrounded by her family, Florence was able to speak,

“Detective, I turned around to see my uncle standing there. He covered my mouth with his hand so I wouldn’t scream, turned me around and burned me with his cigarette several times. He told me if I ever said anything that he would hurt us all.” Florence took a deep breath.

Detective Drew Myers observed everyone in the room and picked up a folder.

“Miss Smith, thank you for coming in today to tell me what happened with your uncle. I would like to share the contents of this folder if you’re ready.”

Everyone sat down again with Riley sitting next to Florence and holding her hand.

The detective opened the folder and explained, “We have enhanced the video and have identified the man running from the park. His name is Willis Jenkins, ex-con with a rap sheet a mile long. When he was in jail, his cellmate was your uncle, Jerry Smith." Detective Myers passed the photo of the suspect to Florence and Riley, who passed it to the other members of her family.

Edward Howard spoke up, "How are the two related in this case? Jerry Smith is still in jail until he comes up for parole. We haven't been contacted yet to come talk to the parole board. Florence and I have always spoken to the board in hopes that he is kept in jail."

The detective looked at everyone in the room and asked, "You mean you weren't notified?"

Everyone looked at each other with a question in their eyes. Florence replied, "Notified?"

"Yes," the detective said, "Jerry Smith was released from jail two weeks ago."

Chapter 19

Jerry Smith pulled his car around the back in the alleyway behind what he thought of as his house. He watched everyone leave earlier. He saw his sister-in-law, that cop, the brat, and the runt leaving and now was the time. He got out of his car and looked around. He had a hat pulled low over his face and sunglasses hiding his eyes. He had his gun under his shirt. With an empty house, he wasn't expecting any trouble, but he was smart and always thinking ahead.

He reached the back door and saw a planter. He looked underneath the planter---nothing. He looked around and saw an ugly plastic frog sitting next to the plant. He looked underneath and saw nothing. Then the frog came apart. There was a top and bottom to the frog. He opened it and there was the key. He laughed. Jerry was smart and no one could fool him.

He didn't see any signs or stickers for an alarm system. He was surprised the cop next door that hadn't talked Janet into installing a system. He unlocked the door and carefully went through the door watching for any movement inside just in case. He stopped inside the back door and listened. No alarm. So far, so good. Making his way into the living room, he passed the kitchen and small dining area. His sister-in-law had fixed the place up. He wondered where she got the money. She never could do anything right, and she was always taking up for those whiny brats. Jerry made his way past two bedrooms and then came to a third one.

He looked around. Damn Janet! She had made this into some type of playroom with a record player, paints on the table and damn library books on bookshelves.

This was his room, “Who the hell does she think she is?” The only way to reach his money in the ceiling was to stand on the bed, which was now gone. Damn it! He looked around, frantic to get that money. He needed it to pay the guys back who gave him the stolen car, or they would kill him. He saw a tall stool in the corner. He bet that would work. Jerry dragged the stool over. He put it in the corner of the room where his bed had been. He counted the ceiling tires and moved the stool under the 2nd tile. He lifted the ceiling tile and reached his hand around. His hand landed on the bag. “Hot damn!” he said. He slid the bag over until it dropped to the floor.

He got off the stool and dragged it back where he got it. No sense in somebody noticing something out of place. He couldn’t take the chance if the nosy cop next door found out he had been released from prison. He walked over and untied the bag. He looked inside and pulled out a stack of 100’s, “Well, hello Mr. Franklin!” Jerry cackled and danced around the room. He then put the stack back into the bag and secured it. He started to lift the bag and heard the sound of a car door closing. He peaked out a small slit in the curtain to see the driveway. They were back.

Florence felt numb. She sat in the passenger seat of Riley’s car as he drove them to her apartment. He glanced at her and held her hand. He was concerned. She looked at Riley and then concentrated on looking forward.

When they all heard that Jerry Smith had been released from

prison, they were stunned.

Detective Myers had found out through a colleague that the detective that normally kept Florence and Edward informed about Jerry Smith's probation had retired. The ball got dropped with the in-house communication. Therefore, no one from the family had been contacted. After talking it through with the detective, Edward decided that he would take the family to his house as he still had a license to carry and would defend his home. Riley and Florence decided that her apartment would be best as they didn't think he knew where it was. They all thought the park was too much of a risk at night to be near the bungalows since that was where the last incident happened.

Hunt was still at the hospital assisting with surgeries. He assured Riley he would bunk at the hospital. Riley's mom picked up Aunt Alice, so she was safe. He had explained the situation and both women were frightened and concerned for Riley, the Smiths and Edward.

Riley made sure the park was closed up tight. He had also talked to Toni to make sure she stayed safe as well as all the people who worked for them. She assured him that the park would be emptied of all employees and security was checking all areas and perimeters of the park.

Riley reached Florence's apartment and pulled into the parking lot. He checked the area and saw it was well lit. He came around to the passenger side and opened the door for Florence. She looked at him and was silent. He took her hand and helped her out of the car.

Once at her apartment, she rummaged in her bag for her key and unlocked the door. She stood very still.

"Florence," Riley said, "Let me check it out, hmm?"

She gazed at Riley and said, "No, let's go in together." Once inside he reached around her and shut the door and engaged the locks. Florence stood there and Riley put his arms around Florence. She reached up and held on tight. She looked up at him with tears rolling down her face and said, "Riley, I'm so sorry. I didn't mean to leave you out. I just didn't want you or anyone else hurt."

He kissed her hand, "Don't you know the only way you can truly hurt me is if you left me?"

Florence put her hands on each side of his face, her eyes bright with tears and replied,

"Riley, why would I ever think about leaving you? I love you."

He laid his hands on top of hers, "Florence Smith, I love you too." Then he kissed her.

Edward Howard had seen to it that Karen and Janet made it safely inside his house.

He went to his gun safe and pulled out what he would need. Just in case Jerry Smith decided to show up, he would be ready. After he made sure the gun safe was secure, he walked into the kitchen to see what the ladies would like for dinner. He saw the beginnings of someone putting a salad together, and he opened the fridge to take out the chicken he was going to make in the air fryer. He had potatoes too that he was going to nuke in the microwave. They would have a nice dinner and he would see to it they were secure. He would engage the alarm and be on watch tonight. It had been a long time since he had been on a stakeout, but once a cop, always a cop.

Janet was probably checking on some paperwork in the office. Every so often she would get an afterhours call from her boss checking a policy for a client.

He was getting the potatoes ready when Karen came into the kitchen. She looked at the salad and said to Ed, “You working on the salad too?”

“No,” he said, “I thought you or your mom started putting that together.”

“Not me,” said Karen, “Maybe mom?”

Ed countered with, “I’m sure she’ll be out of her office soon.”

“Her office?” Karen replied, “She’s not back there.”

“Huh, I’m sure she’s probably changing her clothes then.”

Karen shrugged and walked over to finish the salad and the bottom dropped out of her stomach, “Ed! She left a note on the counter.”

He took the note from Karen, “Guys, I forgot my blood pressure medicine and it will only take a minute. I’m going to the house. I’ll be right back.”

Edward froze and then the cop in him went on alert, “Karen, listen carefully,” He took the gun from his jacket holster, “I’m going out the back. Lock up behind me and engage the alarm.”

“Ed?” Karen began shaking.

“Karen, follow my directions exactly.”

“Yes, Ed.” Karen nodded her head and followed him to the back door. “Karen, now!” Ed eased out of the back door.

Riley turned to face Florence. Their passion was heightened by their declaration of love for one another. He ran his finger down her cheek. She turned her head and kissed his finger. Then she moved her mouth on his as her hands roamed down his chest. He took a deep breath. She looked into his beautiful blue eyes. He looked into her eyes and kissed her, “I love you Florence.”

Teardrops began rolling down her face and Riley kissed her tears.

Florence moved her hands up and down his back, looked at him and said, "I love you too, Riley."

His eyes locked with hers and slowly he kissed her. She deepened the kiss, "Florence," he breathed her name out with a hiss. She moved with him. They fit together perfectly. He was hers. She was his. They were made for each other. Riley exclaimed, "I love you Florence."

She kissed him deeply, "I love you so much."

Riley kissed her and settled with her in sleep. A persistent buzzing noise woke him. He grabbed for his phone on the bedside table and looked at the number.

He answered, "Drew? What's going on?"

Florence began to stir next to him, "Do you know where they're headed?" Florence sat up and looked at Riley. She began to get dressed as Riley was pulling on his pants.

"Edward and Karen are following them? I know they're supposed to let you handle it, but he came into her house and took her by gunpoint."

Riley looked at Florence as she gasped, "No!"

Riley pulled on a shirt and slipped into his tennis shoes. "Well, Drew, you're going to have to arrest us then."

He hung up, grabbed his keys, and followed Florence out the door.

Chapter 20

Jerry Smith pulled into the deserted parking lot on the edge of the Delta. As his headlights swept over the parking lot, he saw a small house with a pier. On the side of the pier he could make out a boathouse with a boat. That was going to be his ticket out of here.

Janet sat next to him in the car, a gun to her head. He turned to her, "Well now Janet. Just what should I do with you, hmm?"

Janet turned away from him, not giving him the satisfaction of seeing tears in her eyes.

She should have married Edward a long time ago. She let her fears get the best of her. She thought of her daughters. If she died tonight, she would miss out on Florence finally finding a second chance at love. Karen would be graduating soon, and she would miss seeing Karen receive her diploma. She should have stayed in Edward's house tonight. She should never have gone to her house. She had made a mistake and now Jerry was going to make her pay.

Janet turned back to Jerry with animosity in her eyes, "Whether you kill me or not, they'll find you. You're going back to prison."

"Oh, Janet, so naive," said Jerry as he hit her across the face with the butt of his gun.

Blood spurted out from a deep cut on Janet's face. Jerry laughed, "Now," he directed her, "out of the car," as he waved the gun towards Janet."

She looked at her surroundings to see if she could make a run for it. Jerry followed her line of thinking and said, "Oh, Janet, I wouldn't be wandering too far. The gators are probably hungry this time of night." He laughed again.

He grabbed the money, which he'd stuffed in a backpack and slipped the straps on his back. He clutched Janet's arm, put the gun to her head and said, "Now, start walking."

Edward and Karen had turned off their lights as the car rolled to a stop before the parking lot to the old, abandoned gas station. It was long gone, swept up by a hurricane. Edward remembered a small house and dock near the gas station. As he was about to make his next move, a police car silently rolled up next to them. They got out of the car and the detective motioned for the officer to stand down, "Look detective," said Edward, "you can arrest me if you want, but I'm going to help take this jackass down. He has Janet at gunpoint. We know he's here. The only place to park is in the parking lot up ahead. My guess is he's going to try to take the boat. There's no telling what he's going to do to Janet, and I have to get there to make sure she's safe."

The detective motioned to the officer and told him to call for back-up. Then he called the Marine Patrol Captain as he watched Riley pull up behind the police car.

"Well," Detective Myers said as Riley and Florence got out of the car. "It's not time for a jubilee folks. You need to allow us to do our jobs."

The detective looked at Edward and motioned for the police

officer to take him to the Marine Patrol Boat that was positioned next to a dock not far from where they were standing.

The detective looked at Riley and the sisters.

Riley spoke up first, "Can I talk to you Drew?" He motioned for Drew to step away from Karen and Florence. "Look, maybe I can help. Let me go out to the pier. He doesn't know me.

He'd think I'd be checking on my boat and maybe we can draw his attention away long enough to get Mrs. Smith to safety." Drew was shaking his head.

"Riley, that's just not going to happen. You may be great at running your business, but this is my business." Riley and the detective heard a muffled scream behind them.

"Well, now looks like we all have business here tonight," said Willis Jenkins, as he held a gun on Florence and Karen.

Jerry was lowering the boat when he heard a noise and raised his gun up towards the house, "Somebody better make themselves known. I got a gun here and I will not hesitate to shoot you."

"Well, hello old buddy," said Willis as he walked down the path to the boathouse with an entourage in front of him holding their hands behind their head.

Jerry asked, "Willis, what are you doing here?"

"Looks like I did you a favor and I thought I'd come for the reward."

"What reward would that be Willis?"

"I followed you Jerry. Saw you waiting down the street from this lady's house," he said, as he pointed to Janet, "I knew something must be up and decided to follow you here. Now, I'm sure you're not going on a late-night picnic with some snacks in that bag," Willis said as he smiled. "So," said Willis, as he stopped smiling. "What's in the bag? Wouldn't happen to be that $100,000.00 you used to talk about, now would it?" As Willis and Jerry continued to talk, Detective Myers noticed a slight movement to his left. Out of the corner of his eye, he saw two police officers with weapons drawn moving silently through the woods. Willis waved his gun as a signal for everyone to move towards the pier, "Let's just take a closer look."

"I wouldn't do that if I were you, Willis. This gun might go off and someone might get killed. Could be you."

Willis answered Jerry, "With all these bodies to choose from out here, you might just miss me and hit one of them. Then I'd have my chance. I don't think I'd miss where I'm standing."

"Fair enough," Jerry moved the gun towards Janet.

Florence cried out, "No, please don't shoot her. Take me instead."

"Florence, no. I'm not going to let you do that," said Riley

Jerry looked closer, "Well, lookie who we got here. It's the theme park guy in that commercial with Florence."

Willis was now close enough to see the bag. He motioned for everyone to sit down on a bench on the pier and held the gun on them. He glanced at the bag and then at Jerry, "Now, toss me the bag." Jerry stared at Willis then threw him the bag. Willis caught the bag, pointed his gun at Jerry and looked inside. He glanced at Jerry and started to laugh, "Well, Jerry, this is where we say goodbye." Willis grabbed Florence and held the gun to her head.

Riley stood up to move towards Willis, "Riley, please no!" begged Florence.

Willis chuckled, "Now ain't that sweet." He looked at the

detective, “No one follows us or I kill her.”

As Willis backed up, Florence tripped on a rock. Jerry swung his gun towards Willis as Riley yelled, “Florence!” and jumped in front of her.

The policemen came out of the woods and Willis, pointing his gun, turned to look at the noise. They fired, striking Willis, and killing him instantly. Drew swung his weapon toward Jerry, but it was too late. Jerry had shot his gun as the Marine Patrol boat swung around and yelled, “Drop your weapon!” Jerry turned around to fire his gun towards the patrol and Edward shot him in the chest. Jerry fell back into the water. He started screaming and splashing as an alligator emerged from behind him. The alligator latched on to him and maneuvered a death roll, submerging him under the water.

Janet and Karen ran towards Florence who was holding Riley. She was screaming and crying, “No! No! Someone please!” Her hands were covered in blood. Riley had been shot in the back by Jerry.

The officers called out to Drew, “The ambulance is already on the way.” Drew was applying pressure to the wound. The Marine patrol had an officer who was a nurse in the military. He grabbed his bag and ran onto the dock. He felt for a pulse. He shook his head at the detective.

“Come on, come on!” The nurse began chest compressions.

Florence cried out, “Riley, come on Riley! You can’t leave me! We’re worth fighting for! Please!”

The nurse signaled, “We got a pulse. Here’s the ambulance.” Florence ran alongside the stretcher as Riley was moved into the ambulance. The medic motioned for her to hop in. The ambulance took off with the medics working on Riley and Florence holding his hand.

Florence was pacing in the hospital lobby waiting for word on Riley. He'd been in surgery for 2 hours now. Hunt had met the ambulance and gone into surgery with him.

Karen had taken Riley's phone from Florence and called his mom. Florence paced back to the chairs where everyone waited. A nurse had taken her to a partitioned room and given her a pair of scrubs to change into as she was covered in Riley's blood. Edward had his arm around Janet, who had her gash on her cheek bandaged by one of the doctors when she had entered the hospital. Karen was sitting next to Aunt Alice and Riley's mom. Drew Myers was standing with his back to one of the columns in the lobby waiting room area.

Karen got up to hug her, "Come sit down, Flo, and rest awhile."

"I can't. I can't sit down until I know he's alright." Florence began to cry and exclaimed to Karen, "I just found him. I can't lose him! "Janet came over to hug her daughter.

Mary, Riley's mom, walked up to the women. Mary asked, "How about Florence and I take a short walk?"

Florence said, "I can't leave him!" She sobbed.

Mary hugged her, "We'll be right over here." Mary walked Florence a short distance away. "We're close enough to hear how he is, okay?" Florence nodded her head.

"I want to thank you for making my son so happy. I've not seen him this happy in a long time. You know when his father died, he hardly said two words to anyone. I was so upset because I felt no matter what I said, nothing helped. As time went on and with Frank and Alice getting him more involved in the park operation, he seemed to get better. He had a purpose and a way to make his dad proud." Tears came into Mary's eyes, "I miss Justin every day, but I see so much of him in Riley. He has grown up to be a wonderful man, but there always seemed to be something missing in his life. Oh, he had the park, but he was missing someone to love besides his mom, uncle, aunt, and Hunt. Now, he has you. And I'll tell you something else. My son has two wonderful men looking out for him," Mary looked up to heaven.

She kissed Florence on the cheek and walked towards Janet. Janet looked up with tears in her eyes and squeezed Mary's hand, "Thank you," she said.

Florence continued to pace and heard something familiar. She heard music and went to stand at the windows looking out to the parking lot. Tears started to fall down her face. She realized it was the song playing the first time she and Riley were together in sharing their love with one another. Two less lonely people in the world...

As the song played, she thought about the first time she met Riley, in that ridiculous clown costume and she smiled through her tears. She thought about all the times she came close to kissing him and laughing with him: when he told her he was her boss and how mad she was; when he watched her dance in the gym; when they danced at Swanson's and how close he held her when they danced in the parade; when he met Curtis and told her how he felt; laughing at his house with Hunt telling his terrible jokes, and loving him that last time at her apartment and the first time they both said, "I love you." Then, the memory of seeing all of the blood and thinking he was dead.

She paced back to the chair next to Karen, put her head down and sobbed. Karen held on to her. She was still sobbing when she felt two arms come around her. She looked up and there was Hunt kneeling in front of her in his scrubs. She heard crying and looked up. Riley's mom was holding Aunt Alice and both women were crying. She glanced back at Hunt, who had tears in his eyes. Tears spilled over from Florence, "No, Hunt, please no." Hunt wiped away her tears, smiled and said, "He's a stubborn bastard!"

Florence looked at Hunt and didn't understand, "What? He's not dead?" asked Florence as a kernel of hope built up inside her, "Everyone's crying," she said.

Hunt held her arms and explained, "Those are happy tears. Mary was the first one I saw when I came out here. She's crying happy tears. It was rough going, Florence." Hunt had tears in his eyes, "We lost him once on the table." Hunt looked around the room at all of the people that loved Riley and Florence, including himself, "Florence, he has many good reasons to live and I think one of the biggest reasons is you. He really loves you."

Florence looked at Hunt and replied, "I love him too. Thank you for saving him." "I didn't do it alone," Hunt remarked, as he pointed towards heaven.

Florence was so happy that she hugged Hunt and almost knocked him over. She laughed through her tears, "Sorry."

He hugged Florence. Hunt looked at the wonderful woman he knew his best friend would spend the rest of his life with and said, "No sorrier than I am. He's a lucky man."

Florence sat by Riley's bed in the Intensive Care Unit. He'd been transferred there from the operating room. She took in the breathing machine and the bags of fluid and medications. She watched the heart monitor with such intensity and felt as if she took her eyes off the machine, it might stop. He was so still. Mary and Aunt Alice had been in earlier to see him.

They were crying when they came back to the lobby area of the hospital but holding each other and smiling through their tears. Mary was taking Aunt Alice back to her house in Pensacola.

They both hugged Florence. Florence had looked up then to see Hunt waiting to take her back to visit Riley. Edward had taken her mom and her sister back to his house. Janet and Edward were talking about getting married and moving into his house or moving to a different neighborhood altogether. Janet didn't want to be reminded of the violence that had occurred in her home.

Florence saw that Detective Myers hadn't moved from where he was standing.

She looked at him and he smiled, gave a thumbs up and left the hospital.

Florence got up from her chair to be closer to Riley. She smoothed down his hair.

She laid her head down close to his shoulder and started to cry when she realized how close she had come to losing him. Florence felt a hand move next to her head. She looked up and saw those big beautiful blue eyes looking at her, "Riley! Oh, Riley!" She cried again, "Oh, it's so good to see you! I thought I'd lost you!" Florence rubbed her cheek against his hand and closed her eyes. When she looked up, he was staring at the opening in the curtain.

Hunt raised his hand as tears moistened his eyes, "Well, hello old man."

Hunt stood next to Florence. He could tell Riley was trying to move his lips. He leaned his ear down to Riley's mouth. Hunt stood and said, "You're welcome. Just don't do it again." Riley's mouth moved. Hunt said, "See, I told you I was funny."

Chapter 21

Hunt looked at the pint-sized witch and filled her plastic pumpkin with treats. He grinned as she thanked him and ran to the next booth.

"Well, aren't you a smart looking Scarecrow," said Florence as she sat next to Hunt at his booth.

"According to the movie, Dorothy, I do get a brain." Her mouth curved as she noticed a lion moving closer to their booth. She took a deep breath and realized it was the perfect costume for Riley. He truly had needed a lot of courage to get through the last couple of months. She was so grateful he was alive and well.

"Looks like a good crowd for the park, doesn't it? Sure doesn't hurt that the sun is shining and the temperature is mild today." Riley bent down to kiss Florence, "Dorothy, you sure are looking pretty this afternoon." He thanked his lucky stars for the two people sitting at this booth. Both had a part in making sure he was alive today.

"You're not looking so bad yourself, Lion." Florence stood up and hugged Riley. She closed her eyes and held him tightly.

"Okay, you all, make room for the Good Witch," Toni sauntered up to the group wearing a beautiful pink ball gown fit for a queen.

Florence said, "Toni, you look absolutely beautiful! We've got the whole group here except our Tin Man. Anyone know where he is?" She heard someone clear their throat behind her,

"He's right here." Florence looked up into the face of Drew Myers. At least, she thought it was Drew under the silver paint.

"Hello, Drew. Your costume is very good."

He held out his arms to reveal a man dressed in a silver costume from his tin hat down to his gray boots that covered his feet, "Let's just hope this silver paint comes off before I have to go to work on Monday."

Riley laughed, "Just think how festive you'll look if it doesn't!" Drew rolled his eyes. Hunt gazed at the group, "Aren't we missing someone?"

They noticed the Wicked Witch fly up to the group. Karen got off the golf cart resembling a flying monkey, looked at the driver and said, "Thank you, Cecil." He nodded as he zipped back to the float barn. She smiled at everyone. She picked up her Halloween bag filled with treats. "Flo, how about Dorothy and the Wicked Witch have a truce long enough to hand out candy?" Florence grinned and sighed, "Why, not?"

Just then a cowgirl ran up to Florence, "Hi Miss Smith!"

"Frances! Your costume looks great!" Florence glanced at one of her favorite students who came regularly to the park for the education sessions. Dressed from head to toe in a bright blue cowgirl outfit with a hat and matching boots, she was a sight to behold.

Riley joined Florence, "Well, howdy Miss Frances. How are you?"

Frances looked up at Riley, "Hi Mr. Riley. My outfit matches your pretty blue eyes."

Those pretty blue eyes crinkled, and he replied, "Well, Miss Frances, I really appreciate that. Why don't you pick something out from Miss Smith's bag? She's got a lot of good stuff in there. Then you need to see the Wicked Witch next." Both Florence and Karen held out their bags.

Frances picked out a few pieces of candy. She turned and waved to a lady behind her, "Be right there!" This was Frances's foster mother. Florence and Riley glanced at each other. She seemed like a perfectly nice lady and Frances seemed okay. She was almost nine years old and they would like to see her in a permanent home.

Frances gazed up at Riley, "Thank you, Mr. Riley."

He looked at her and smiled, "One more thing, Miss Frances. Can't have a cowgirl costume without this." Riley revealed a shiny silver sheriff's star, "Oh, Mr. Riley! Look Miss Florence!"

Florence glanced at the man she loved, and her mouth curved, "Frances, would you like me to pin it on?" "Yes, Miss Smith! Please!" She pinned it on Frances.

Riley was almost knocked over when Frances ran to him for a big hug. He laughed. "Bye, now!" They grinned as Frances ran to the next booth.

"Bongo!" Riley looked around and there was Scott Williams and his father, Jacob, dressed as Luke Skywalker and Obi Wan Kenobi.

Riley squatted down in front of Scott, "How did you know it was me?" "I'd recognize your color of eyes anywhere. Where's the clown?"

Jacob handed Riley the key ring of icons and picked out a picture of a man eating dinner. "Oh, shoot, he's eating food!

When can I see him?"

"Scott, next time ask your dad to let me know when you're coming to the park, and I'll ask Bongo to come for a visit. Okay?"

He held out his fist to Riley and they bumped fists. Scott held out his lightsaber. "Well, the force must be strong with this one." said Tori, as she joined the group.

She looked at her costume and at Jacob. His gaze roamed over her costume, and he grinned. Florence's eyes sparkled as she spoke up, "Did you all call each other to arrange this?"

Tori looked at her Princess Leia costume and just shook her head. Scott moved over closer to Tori, looked up at her with his big blue eyes and breathed, "Princess Leia! You came! You're the other lady who helps my dad."

Tori smiled and gave him a fist bump, "Hey, Scott, I like that costume!"

"Thanks! My dad and I worked and worked on what to wear." The group grinned at Scott's excitement, "After taking forever and ever, dad said for the love of God, just pick one!" Everyone laughed. Jacob's eyes showed laughter too as he put his hand on Scott's shoulder.

"Okay, Luke Skywalker, how about we go get some candy?"

His eyes widened and he asked, "I can have candy tonight?" Jacob smiled and nodded his head. "All right! Princess Leia, you can go too."

He took her hand and pulled her after him. "Looks like I'm going with y'all." Tori's mouth curved.

Jacob's eyes caught hers and he replied, "Yep." He was glad she would be spending time with her and thanked God for his son's impulsiveness. Jacob laughed to himself and caught up with Tori. Scott visited every booth at warp speed. Tori and Jacob were breathless when Scott stopped at the last booth. They all sat at a picnic table so he could empty his bag and pick out his favorite candy to eat. He looked at his dad, who held up 3 fingers. Scott looked over all the candy intently and finally picked out three pieces of candy.

Tori smiled. Jacob gazed at her and winked. He looked over at the food booth. "Scott, would you like something to drink?"

He looked at the big pictures of drinks on the board. "Dad, how about a hot chocolate?" Jacob nodded. "Tori, may I get you anything?" Scott eyed Tori.

She gazed at him, "I'll take hot chocolate too. Thank you." Scott grinned. Tori's heart melted at that smile.

"Three hot chocolates, coming right up!" Jacob left to get the drinks,

Scott looked at Tori and handed her three pieces of candy. She handed one back. "Trade you this one for a chocolate milky way." She waited. Scott glanced at his candy and back at Tori. He sighed and handed over the candy bar. Her eyes twinkled. "Thank you, Scott. These are my favorite! "He glanced at her and stuck up his thumb. She grinned. Jacob returned with the drinks.

Tori's eyes widened as she glanced at the steaming cup of hot chocolate topped with a frothy scoop of whipped cream with chocolate drizzled all over topped by a chocolate bar. "That's some serious looking drink right there. I'll have to get in more steps to justify having this."

Jacob gazed at Tori in her costume, "You shouldn't have to do much." A smile reached his eyes as her mouth curved. She gazed at Jacob as she sipped her hot chocolate. He really was cute with that blonde hair and those blue eyes that reminded her of the ocean. Tori sighed as she had a thing about dating clients.

Scott's dad glanced at Tori more than once tonight. He thought she was a very striking woman with her long dark hair and beautiful mahogany skin. Jacob hadn't dated anyone since the divorce as all his energy had been reserved for his son. It'd be nice to take someone to dinner or to go to a movie every once in a while. He'd have to work on that.

"Scott, since there's no school tomorrow, do you want to go on some rides?" His eyes widened.

. "You mean we can play tonight?" He pumped his fist in the air. "Let's go!" They helped Scott put all his candy back in his bag and zipped it up. It was a fun end to an evening as all three of them hopped on roller coasters, water rides and visited the farm. Jacob was holding a sleeping Scott as Tori walked with them to the car.

He buckled him in and turned to her as she handed over his bag, "I had a great time tonight. I'm glad you joined us," said Jacob.

She looked into those blue eyes and reminded herself not to do anything crazy, "Me too."

He took her hand and let out a breath. Tori stared at him for a minute, but then moved into his arms. His embrace was heavenly, making her realize it was the first hug she had in a long while. Jacob enjoyed the feeling of hugging a woman again, especially this woman.

He reminisced about their time together as children and it seemed new memories were on the horizon with her beginning tonight. Jacob cleared his throat and drew himself away from her. She smiled at him and he moved his hand to rub the back of his neck, "Well, I better be getting Scott home. Wait, where are you parked? I want to make sure you get to your car safely."

"I'm all the way on the other side of the park, but I'll be fine." She shrugged him off.

"Nonsense. What kind of Jedi Master would I be if I didn't make sure you got to your car okay?" He looked at his car and smirked, "It's no Delta 7 starfighter, but it'll get you where you need to be."

She glanced his way and said, "Well, the force must be strong with you too." Jacob looked at her and chuckled.

Chapter 22

.

It was a clear November night in Alabama, a balmy 75 degrees with no rain in sight, with a nice breeze rolling through the trees. Riley had asked Florence to meet him by the Ferris wheel. She shuddered when she thought back to that horrible night, the thought of losing him terrified her. It had been a rough couple of months for Riley. He was in the hospital for three weeks with time in recovery and rehab, with Florence visiting him daily. Physical therapy and getting his strength back had taken a toll on him, but he persevered. Hunt had later shared with her that the bullet fired by Jerry Smith had just missed his spinal cord. She was just grateful to have him back again.

"Well, Miss Smith, fancy meeting you here on such a beautiful night."

Florence turned at the sound of that melodic voice and looked into those beloved blue eyes, "Well, Mr. Simmons, it seems like I got an offer too good to refuse." Florence walked into Riley's arms and held on tight. His lips grazed the top of her head. He looked at the face he thought he'd never see again. Riley kissed Florence.

He never wanted this night to end, "Florence Smith," said Riley. "I have summoned you here as I thought you might want to take a ride with a handsome man."

Florence looked around, "Sure, will he be here soon?"

Riley grinned at her and said, "Smartass." She smirked. They filed onto the Ferris wheel, with Riley offering his arm for support as she hoisted herself inside the car. He pressed the remote, and they began to climb up into the sky. She held onto his arm and rested her head on his shoulder. Riley held her hand. He stopped the car midway up. They gazed at the wonderful view of the park.

She asked, "Riley, you really love this park, don't you?"

Riley looked at Florence and squeezed her hand, "I do." He leaned over and kissed her, "Yes, Florence, I have loved this park for as long as I can remember."

She looked at him and squeezed his hand, "I have a question for you, Riley." Riley kissed her hand, "Ask away."

"Do you think after we're married that we'll still live in the park?"

Riley said, "Well, I think…." He stopped mid-sentence trying to process the words coming out of Florence, "What did you say?"

"I said….", Riley held a finger to her lips, "Florence, do you absolutely know how much I love you? Do you know how happy I am being with you?"

Florence kissed Riley's finger then leaned forward to meet his mouth with hers. He intensified the kiss and held her close.

When Florence could take a breath, she said to Riley, "You haven't answered my question." His eyes roamed over the park and thought what a wonderful life they could have here with each other. They could build a family here. He looked up towards heaven and smiled.

"Riley, what's your answer?" Riley moved within inches

from Florence's face. He gazed into her eyes and then looked at her mouth, kissing her.

"Yes. My answer is yes," he replied, as he slid something on her finger.

"Riley!" Florence cried out as she looked at the silver band with the small diamond.

"Florence, this is the engagement ring my father gave to my mother, on this very same Ferris wheel 30 years ago and now, I want to give it to you as a symbol of my love." A tear fell from Riley's eye. He cleared his throat and said, "I love you Florence, with all my heart." Tears flooded Florence's eyes, "Riley Simmons, I love you too." Riley kissed her.

Florence asked, "Riley?"

"Yes, Florence?" Riley breathed.

"I think we have an audience." They looked down. All of the people who were family were below the Ferris wheel clapping and whistling. Aunt Alice and his mom, Mary were there. Her sister Karen and her mom, Janet, Edward, and Hunt. They were all there to share Riley and Florence's engagement. Riley looked at her with love shining in his eyes. He picked up the remote to lower the car and said, "Ready?"

Florence smiled at the man who had shown her that you can love again. Florence said, "Yes, Riley. I'm ready."

Epilogue

It was a beautiful November weekend for a wedding. The sun had risen in the sky that morning giving warmth to a crisp fall day. Riley was standing in the dancer's circle at the top of Sunshine Street. He was dapper in navy tails with a cream-colored rose on his lapel. He looked at Hunt, his best man who stood beside him in a tan tailored suit. He glanced behind him at the float decorated with flowers. He spotted the name of the float, The Wedding Bouquet. He smiled.

Riley had closed the park for the day.

He observed those around him. Riley saw employees and friends lined up on either side of Sunshine Street. Florence's mom and Edward were standing next to his mom, Aunt Alice and her best friend, Elmira. Toni, Fred, Rafael, and Kevin were all in attendance. Hunt's parents, Oliver and Annie Huntington had just flown in from a church mission trip in time for the wedding. Riley had spotted Tori in the crowd standing next to Jacob, Scott's father. He had even reached out to a family to see if they would want to be a part of this special day. They had immediately said they would be happy to attend the wedding. Riley saw a movement near his family and looked up to see Detective Drew Myers. Everyone who was special to Florence and Riley were all there.

He heard the music begin. The reverberation of violins, oboes and flutes filled the air.

Riley turned as the beveled glass doors opened. He saw Frances walking towards him dropping rose petals. She had become very special to Florence and him. He winked at her and she winked back. Riley grinned. Scott, another little boy who had charmed them all, followed Frances carrying the wedding rings on a small pillow. He did as he practiced and stood next to Hunt. Scott let out a big breath. Hunt smiled at him. Karen, the maid of honor, dressed in a beautiful blue chiffon gown, walked towards the circle. Riley's mouth curved as she stood next to Frances.

Turning back to look at the doors, their eyes locked. His heart was full. He had never seen anyone as beautiful as Florence as she advanced his way. The ball gown wedding dress fit her silhouette perfectly as she stepped towards him. To Riley she looked like a queen and then there she was. His future wife was standing before him. As Florence gave her bouquet to Karen, he took her hand and turned towards the dear old Irish priest, Father James Murphy.

As the music continued to play, Father Murphy winked at them both and began the ceremony, "Dearly beloved, we are gathered here today…" Standing before Father Murphy, they said their vows and pledged their love to each other. Hunt reminded Scott to move forward. Florence gave him a fist bump after he handed over the rings. With a promise in their eyes of a lifetime together, they slipped the rings on each other's fingers. They glanced at Father Murphy with joy on their faces. The old Irish priest blessed them and spoke up, "Now Riley and Florence, this is the best part.

Go ahead and give each other a kiss, as now you're good and married."

They turned to one another. Riley put his hand on his bride's cheek, leaned in and kissed her. Florence covered his hand with her own. Everyone clapped and cheered. Riley looked at Florence and whispered, "I hope you don't mind, but I would like to give you a gift."

Florence touched his face and asked, "Now?"

Riley looked at her with love and answered, "Yes." He kissed her hand. "The night you were injured at the park, you came into my home and you gave me a precious gift which I will cherish always. You gave of yourself. I would now like to give you a gift. I love you Florence." Riley had Florence sit on a bench placed behind them. He sat next to her.

As the music continued with violins soaring, Hunt winked at Riley and handed him a microphone. There was a hush in the crowd. Riley looked at Florence and began to sing along to the music, "When I am down, and, oh, my soul so weary, When troubles come, and my heart burdened be, Then, I am still and wait here in the silence, Until you come and sit awhile with me. You raise me up, so I can stand on mountains, You raise me up to walk on stormy seas.

I am strong when I am on your shoulders, You raise me up to more than I can be."

The music continued. As tears rolled down her face, Florence stood up with Riley, touched his cheek, "Riley Simmons, what a beautiful voice and what a beautiful gift. Thank you." He kissed her and said, "Anytime." Florence kissed him back, "Let's go see the family and some friends before we have our dance. He caressed her face, "We aren't done yet, Mrs. Simmons." She smiled and kissed him.

As he tucked her hand in the crook of his arm, they walked towards their families.

Florence worked her way down the line hugging and greeting everyone as Riley walked behind her. She took a step and stopped. She looked back at Riley and he smiled. There before her were the Daltons: Mr. and Mrs. Dalton, Keith's sister, Leslie and her brother, Curtis.

Mrs. Dalton put her hand over her heart and hugged Florence, who had tears falling down her face. Mr. Dalton kissed her on the cheek and smiled at her. Keith's sister gave her a big hug and laughed through her tears and then there was Curtis. His eyes shone with unshed tears as he hugged her. He said, "Keith would be so proud of the woman you have become, and he would be so glad you found someone who loves you." Then Curtis looked at Riley, "You take care of her. She's very special to us."

Riley glanced at Curtis and stuck his hand out. Curtis shook his hand. Riley spoke up,

"I've got an idea for the Founding Farmers area and would like your input. Maybe you wouldn't mind coming to the park to talk about it sometime."

Curtis looked from Florence to Riley and saw how happy they were. He replied, "I think we can make that happen." He nodded to them both, "Congratulations."

Florence and Riley finished greeting everyone and he turned to her, "Ready for our dance?"

She asked, "Here?"

"Yes," said Riley, as he pointed to the float.

She put her hands on her face and cried for joy, "Josh Groban! You got Josh Groban to sing?"

Riley smiled, "Yes, he owed me a favor." Riley then bowed, "Mrs. Simmons, may I have the honor of this dance?"

Florence curtsied, "Why, yes, Mr. Simmons, I'd be honored." As Josh Groban continued to sing, Florence and Riley danced their first dance. The couple glided in front of the float.

It was a cliché, but Florence really did feel like Cinderella. When the song and dance were over, they boarded the float and thanked their special guest. He nodded, took the wedding favor offered and walked off the float grinning.

Hunt and Karen met them on the float with Frances and Scott. The float moved down the main street. Riley and Florence smiled and waved to all their friends and loved ones, as the group on the float tossed wedding favors to celebrate the day. He leaned over to his bride and kissed her as the float circled back to the Hospitality Center.

The happy couple hugged their loved ones as they entered the building. Riley and Florence were so surprised by how beautifully the center was decorated for their wedding. White linen covered tables held beautiful red, orange, and yellow flowers. A cascade of balloons with the bride and groom's colors floated over the wedding cake table. The wedding cake was pure elegance. The groom's cake had been chosen by Hunt as a gift to his best friend. The layers of the treehouse spiraled upwards. Framed pictures of Riley's dad and uncle surrounded his cake. Aunt Alice and Riley's mom brushed by the groom's cake table and smiled at the pictures. Mary picked up a picture of her husband. She kissed her fingers and pressed it to the picture. Aunt Alice smiled fondly at Frank. She missed him tremendously. He would have had fun here this evening. Riley met his mom and aunt at the cake table. When he saw the treehouse cake he grinned. He kissed his mom and hugged Aunt Alice. His aunt wiped the tears from his eyes and told him this was a happy day.

"I know, Aunt Alice. I just miss them so much." Mary

hugged her son.

Hunt headed over to the table, "Nice treehouse." His eyes crinkled and he laughed.

Riley stared at his best friend and gave him a hug, "Thanks man. I don't know what I'd do without you."

Hunt hugged him back, "I know! Who would tell you all the latest jokes if you didn't have me?"

Riley replied, "Someone funny?" They both looked at each other and grinned.

Florence joined the group and took Riley by the hand, "If you will excuse us please. I believe I need the groom to help me cut the cake, and I need all of you to join us please." Florence smiled at the group as she walked hand-in-hand with her husband to cut their cake. The couple fed each other a piece of cake and toasted each other with champagne. Everyone visited with each other and ate and drank heartily before sampling the wedding cake.

At one point, Hunt clinked his glass with a spoon and stood by the groom's cake holding a glass of champagne, "It's time to toast my best friend and his kind and beautiful bride. I would like to share a poem."

"We've been best friends since knee-high,

With treehouses to climb to watch the stars in the sky. We'd fight, we'd laugh, like friends usually do.

I've met other people, but no one like you.

You work in a park and make people happy all day. I treat people who are ill, so they will feel okay.

We were two, but now there's another. She's yours to love, as you have discovered. Today, you both took vows and then pledged your love,

And this union was blessed by those in heaven above.

You might wonder why I've added no humor to this toast today.

I wondered myself, but I think that's okay. To Riley and Florence, we all raise our glass. I'm so glad you found each other, together at last."

Hunt wiped his tears then sipped from his glass. There was a hush in the room.

He looked around. One by one, everyone stood up and clapped. He smiled with tears still in his eyes. He put his glass on the table and wiped his eyes. When he turned, Riley was there. Hunt spoke up and said, "Man, we need to shut off these waterworks. It was just a poem. Jesus!" He grinned at Riley as they clasped each other's shoulders.

Florence joined Riley. She stepped up to Hunt and kissed him on the mouth, "That's for making me cry at my wedding."

Hunt's eyes widened, "I'll never wash these lips again."

Florence hugged him with a smile in her eyes and said, "That was funny, Hunt. Good for you."

Riley snickered and took Florence in his arms, "Hello, Mrs. Simmons. Would you like to dance?" She patted Hunt on the shoulder and told him thank you for the poem. "Yes, Mr. Simmons, I would love to dance with you."

He waved to them both and said aloud, "Always a best man, never a groom." He smiled as he went to ask Aunt Alice to dance.

Jacob looked across the room at Tori. She was stunning in a

red dress. He noticed that it hugged her in all of the right places. Those thoughts were probably not good to be thinking since she was a professional helping his son, but he couldn't help it. Tori glanced up at Jacob and met his eyes. If she wasn't mistaken, she noticed interest there. Hating the rule at this moment that she made to herself about not dating clients, she decided it wouldn't hurt to ask him to dance.

Tori gazed at Jacob in a dark blue suit that fit him just right, "Hi, Jacob. Would you like to dance?"

Jacob eyed Tori and took her hand, "Yes, I'd like that very much." As they turned to each other on the dance floor, Toni watched from her table.

Riley joined her, "Looks like romance is in the air," Riley commented.

Toni responded, "They do make a beautiful couple. They sure were cute playing together when they were little. Who knew they would cross paths as adults?" She put her hand on Riley's, "It was a beautiful wedding. I'm so happy for you and Florence."

He leaned over and kissed her on the cheek, "Thank you for being such a good friend and for holding down the fort for us while we're on our honeymoon."

Toni patted his cheek. "You two have fun in the TreeHouse. Does Florence know yet?" Riley grinned, "No, it's a surprise."

She picked up her glass and toasted him, "You two have a good week and don't worry about a thing."

Riley touched her hand, "Thanks, Toni." He walked over to join his bride, who was visiting with Fr. Murphy and Hunt. At the request of Annie and Oliver Huntingdon, Father Murphy was asked to lead an Irish dance. As the guests all followed his lead, the old Irish priest was nimble on his feet, stepping lively to the

Irish music played by the band hired for the wedding.

Afternoon turned to dusk for those celebrating the love of a special couple. The wedding cake had been devoured, the champagne bottles were emptied, and coffee had been offered to those about to embark outdoors on a cool November night. Gifts were piled high and would be moved to Florence's apartment for the couple to open another time. Riley and Florence thanked everyone for coming and moved to the doors. It was time for Riley and Florence to leave.

Everyone lined up outside of the Hospitality Center and cheered Riley and Florence as they ran through the bubbles. Walking hand-in-hand, they left the crowd of family and friends behind to make their way through the park. Riley lifted one of Florence's hands and kissed it. She then proceeded to move closer and kissed him.

He kissed her back and said, "Mrs. Simmons, have I told you in the last 5 minutes how much I love you?"

"Well, Mr. Simmons, it's been more like ten minutes, but then, who's counting?"

Riley gazed at Florence and said, "I am. I'm counting on all of the wonderful years we have to look forward to."

Florence kissed Riley, "Mr. Simmons, am I going to have somewhere to sleep tonight?"

Riley turned Florence around as they reached their destination. Riley asked his beautiful bride, "Mrs. Florence Simmons, how do you feel about treehouses?"

The End

About the Author

Debbie McDonald grew up in Mobile, AL, the youngest of seven children. She has many fond memories of spending time over the bay in the old cinder block house!

Living in Daphne, AL gives much access to the Eastern Shore and Mobile Bay with the terrific view of the water and beautiful sunsets! She is a wife, mother and pet owner. She has worked as an Educator for 32 years! Debbie began her writing career in college at the University of South Alabama when her essay was chosen to be included in an English class textbook. She received a check for $25 and a copy of the textbook. It was a highlight of her college career! Over thirty years later, life's experiences led her to write her first book of romantic fiction with more to come in the Over the Bay Series!

Made in the USA
Monee, IL
20 April 2021

65245919R00121